IMMOBILITY

TOR BOOKS BY BRIAN EVENSON

Dead Space: Martyr
Immobility

IMMOBILITY

BRIAN EVENSON

TOR®

A TOM DOHERTY ASSOCIATES BOOK
NEW YORK

IMMOBILITY

Copyright © 2012 by Brian Evenson

A Tor Book
Published by Tom Doherty Associates, LLC
175 Fifth Avenue
New York, NY 10010

www.tor-forge.com

Tor® is a registered trademark of Tom Doherty Associates, LLC.

ISBN 978-0-7653-3096-3 (hardcover)
ISBN 978-1-4299-9288-6 (e-book)

First Edition: April 2012

Printed in the United States of America

0 9 8 7 6 5 4 3 2 1

For Peter Wessel Zapffe
and Thomas Ligotti;
and for Greb, always

And for Kristen Tracy

In the true movement of community what is at stake is never humanity, but always *the end of humanity*.

—Jean-Luc Nancy

It is the desire and goal of the Church to gather and preserve copies of the world's genealogical information recorded through the ages into one central storage area where they will be safe from the ravages of nature and the destructions of man. . . . The magnificent machinery is in motion, and in an efficient, businesslike manner, page by page and book by book these records are being stored as priceless treasures, securely protected in the tops of the mountains.

—Brother Sidney B. Sperry

Infinite emptiness will be all around you, all the resurrected dead of all the ages wouldn't fill it, and there you'll be like a little bit of grit in the middle of the steppe.

—Samuel Beckett, *Endgame*

PART ONE

A SENSATION OF COMING BACK alive again, only not quite that, half life maybe. Still utter darkness, though perhaps a faint hint of light on the horizon. Scraps and bits of sound caught somewhere between brain and ears and slowly unthawing to become words, trickling slowly in, but in such a way that it is hard to be sure if they are words from now or words remembered from an earlier time, things imagined or things actually heard. The word food, *or perhaps* brood. *Dying out or crying out, something of the sort, hard to say which exactly, if either.* Claps? *No, not that exactly, but* Claps *still sparked something, was close to something else.* Clasp? Lapse?*

The darkness bedappled now, but still nothing visible, figures not yet sufficiently separated from the ground to become distinct. A dripple, a strange sensation, intimations of shape and form and movement. Almost like being alive again.

And then, suddenly, sentences. Murky but comprehensible and properly sequenced—probably real for once rather than imagined. This:

. . .

"WELL, WE'LL HAVE TO USE HIM, then."

A male voice, hoarse and loud.

"Do you think that's a good idea?"

Another man, this one perhaps younger. The voice, at the very least smoother, more quiescent.

"Do we have any other choice?"

"How do we manage the situation?"

"I'll come up with something."

"What?" The voices getting softer now, slipping down in pitch, starting to fade.

"I don't know." A long silence. "I'll figure something out. We'll just do the best we can."

"So, you want me to wake him?"

A hesitation so long that the conversation seemed over. And then finally:

"Yes, wake him."

SLOW SHIFT TO WHITE NOISE. *Probably a remembered conversation rather than something he was actually hearing, but from when? And who was speaking? Were they even talking about him? If they were talking about him and he was asleep, how could he have heard them? And if they weren't, why did he continue to have the impression that they were?*

Strange the things that seep their way down to you while you are dead, *part of him thought.* Or is it just my imagination? *another part wondered.* A story he was telling himself, a dream he was dreaming.

And who exactly do I mean by *he? he wondered.* Don't I mean *I?* Who do I mean?

And then came a light so bright that, despite just having begun to find himself, he was lost again.

1

WHEN THEY FIRST WOKE HIM, he had the impression of the world becoming real again and he himself along with it. He did not remember having been stored. He could remember nothing about what his life had been before the Kollaps, and the days directly before they had stored him were foggy at best, little more than a few frozen images. He remembered tatters of the Kollaps itself, had a fleeting glimpse of himself panting and in flight, riots, gunfire, rubble. He remembered a bright blast, remembered awakening to find himself burned and naked as a newborn—or perhaps even more naked, since all the hair had been singed from his body or had simply fallen out. He remembered feeling amazed to be alive, but, well, he was alive, it was hard to question that, wasn't it?

And then what? People: he had found them, or they had found him, hard to say which. A few men banded together, acting "rationally" instead of "like animals," as one of them must have put it, attempting to found a new society, attempting to start over.

Not having learned better, he thought grimly, *the first time.*

Was it all coming back to him? He wasn't sure. And how much of what was coming back was real?

What was his name again?

AT FIRST HE COULDN'T FEEL his body at all. He heard noise around him, the low rumble of ordinary mortals muttering to one another, the scuff of feet against a floor around what must be his receptacle. He tried to move his mouth and found he couldn't, that he couldn't even feel it, that he wasn't even completely certain that he had a mouth. It made him nervous. He tried to lick his lips, but either nothing happened or something happened that he couldn't feel.

His eyelids were closed, but there was the slightest gap between them. He could just see out, could see light, a slight blurriness of semi-differentiated figures, nothing more. He tried to will his eyes open further, failed. Nor could he move the eyes themselves: they stayed staring, fixed, his mind very clumsily processing the thin slit of reality available to them.

He tried to swallow, but couldn't move his throat. *Am I breathing?* he wondered, but figured that no, he was in storage, he wasn't breathing, wouldn't breathe until he was fully awake. Assuming he understood the process properly, he was still frozen. He shouldn't be experiencing anything at all yet, shouldn't even be able to think. Why could he?

Horkai, he thought suddenly. *Josef Horkai.* That was his name. It came, flashing back and forth and painfully through him. He tried to keep hold of the name, tried to wrap it around himself and tie it in place with something else, some other fact, anything.

Horkai, he thought. *Occupation? Before the Kollaps? Now?*

Nothing came. *Be patient,* he told himself. *Let things come as they will.*

And then the name flopped away, vanished in darkness.

He tried again to blink, and one eyelid closed fully and held there. The other remained as it was, slit open, but the pupil behind it began to slide, smearing away the little bit of blurred vision he had and coming to rest against the backlit inside of the lid.

He sensed something on the horizon, in the vague redness, coming toward him. His eyelid slid open a little, but he couldn't tell if he had done it or if it had been done to him.

And then there was a roaring and what was coming arrived and turned out to be pain, madly beating its wings. He hurt like hell, every part of him, and since he could not tell where he ended and the rest of the world began, it felt like the entire world was awash in fire. And still he couldn't move, couldn't cry out, couldn't take air into his lungs, nothing. It was terrible, as terrible as anything he had ever felt.

And then slowly it receded, melted away, leaving in its wake a slow twisting and turning of naked sensation that refused to drain off. He could feel parts of himself now, though those parts still felt awkward and dampened, as if wrapped in gauze. One of his eyes sprang open and he could see a blurred thumb and forefinger sheathed in latex holding the eyelids apart. Behind and past them, an arm and vague shapes, several of them, that he guessed to be human. Similar to human, anyway. And then suddenly a blazing circle of light.

"Pupil contracts," he heard someone say. A male voice, hoarse, similar to the one he had heard earlier. "Vision's probably okay."

The blazing circle disappeared, its afterimage tracking across his vision and the figures resolved briefly into being. And then the thumb and forefinger let go and he saw only the inside of his eyelid again.

"What was that?" asked someone new, in a distracted voice.

None of the voices sounded familiar. Then again, why should they?

"I said," the first voice said, louder this time, "that he'll probably be able to see."

"That's not what you said."

"*Vision's probably okay,* I said. Amounts to the same thing."

"Have it your way," said the other. "Hand me the hypodermic."

Silence. And then all at once the remnants of sensation that had been eddying seemed about to burst. All his nerves burned at once. He tried to scream but nothing came out.

He lay there immobile, certain he was dying, until, mercifully, like a candle, he was snuffed out.

2

"HOW ARE WE FEELING?" a voice asked.

His body felt distinct, like a body again, more or less, though tender, sore all over. He willed his eyelids to open, was surprised when they obeyed. His eyes, though, took a long time to adjust. Gradually a blurred figure became distinct, human. A middle-aged man wearing a soiled white technician's coat.

"How are we feeling?" the man asked again, smiling, perhaps two feet away from his face.

He tried to speak, but his tongue was stuck to the roof of his mouth and wouldn't move. He grunted.

The technician squinted and brought his face closer, his eyes lost in a web of wrinkles. Then his face relaxed, grew smooth.

"You'll have to forgive me," the technician said. He reached down, came back up with a bottle of something, a long glass tube running out one end of it. "You'll have to excuse me," he said. "It's been a long time since we've unstored someone."

The technician forced the tube into his mouth. He felt it scrape against his lips, then burrow its way in between his palate and his tongue. It felt like layers of tissue were being torn off. Something was seeping out of the tube, a liquid of some sort, slightly bitter to the taste. Slowly, his tongue loosened, then became independent of the vault of the mouth. The liquid trickled its way deeper into his mouth, down his throat, down his windpipe as well. For a moment, he felt he was choking. He began to cough.

The technician withdrew the tube, helped him to turn his head to the side until the liquid had oozed out and the coughing had stopped. A strand of the fluid hung, black and ropy, from one corner of his mouth.

"There now," said the technician, wiping it away. "All better."

"Hardly," he muttered.

His voice was cracked, his vocal cords having difficulty making the right sounds. The technician looked at him quizzically. He cupped his ear with one hand and leaned in. "You'll have to repeat that," he said.

"Who am I?" he asked.

The technician drew back. "Who are you?" he asked. "Yes, I should have asked that—part of the procedure, just to make sure you came out all right. So, yes, who are you?" the technician asked, and waited.

He shook his head. It felt like his brain was sloshing against the sides of his skull. "No," he said, his voice a little firmer now. "I'm asking you to tell me."

"Who do *you* think you are?"

"I don't know," he said.

"I'll give you a hint," claimed the technician. "I'll give you the first letter."

"Just tell me," he said.

"You start with an *H*," said the technician, leaning closer, rubbing his hands. "It's better this way. It needs to come back to you on its own. That's in the manual."

"Just tell me," he said again.

"After *H,* the next letter is—," the technician started to say to him, but by that time, almost without him knowing it, his hands had found their way to the technician's throat and were squeezing, the man's face darkening.

What am I doing? he wondered in amazement, and let go.

The technician stumbled backwards, hacking and coughing, until he slammed into the wall and slid slowly down.

"My name," he said again.

"Hork eye," the technician gasped.

Horkai, he thought. Yes, that sounded right. Plausible, at least. Close enough, anyway. For now.

THE TECHNICIAN STAYED pressed against the far wall, rubbing his throat, regarding him warily. Horkai had managed to prop himself up on his elbows, but it hadn't been easy. With each movement he'd been struck by a new burst of pain, the last one so bad he had nearly passed out.

He was on a table. Plastic or plasticine, sturdy and long. *Why can I remember what a table is when I can't even remember my own name?* he marveled. He brushed the tabletop with his fingers lightly, feeling its dimpling, but even that simple sensation was almost too much to bear.

In a moment, he told himself, *once I've gathered myself, once I feel okay, I'll swing my legs off the table and stand up. Only not quite yet.*

"You could have killed me," said the technician, his face pale and appalled.

"I'm sorry if things got out of hand," said Horkai. "I didn't mean to hurt you."

"If you didn't mean to hurt me, why were you strangling me?"

Horkai closed his eyes. He shrugged, then winced.

"You're dangerous. They were right to store you," said the technician. "But they weren't right to wake you up."

Horkai didn't bother to respond. "Tell me where I am," he said.

"You're here," said the technician. "Where you've always been."

"Where's here?"

The technician didn't answer.

"Shall I come over there and make you answer?" asked Horkai.

The technician smirked. "Empty threat," he said. "Even I know you can't manage that."

Horkai pressed his lips together. Carefully, he rocked his weight onto one elbow, shifting from the opposite elbow to his hand. The pain made him groan. He rocked the other direction, forced himself onto that hand as well.

The technician looked worried. "I wouldn't do that if I were you," he said.

Horkai ignored him. He tested his arms. They were both weak, atrophied, but would, he thought, support him. He gathered his weight on his arms, swung his legs and body out off the table.

Only his legs wouldn't hold, wouldn't move at all, in fact. They splayed and collapsed, and his forehead glanced off the table next to his own just before he struck the floor hard, pain shooting through his ribs and hip.

He lay there on the floor, staring at a brushed metal table leg. He reached up and touched his head, brought his hand away and saw fingers grown slick with blood.

"You're paralyzed, Horkai," the technician said. "A paraplegic. Don't you remember?" Horkai turned and saw that the technician was now standing. "I'd help you up," the man said, "but I'm afraid to get close to you." And then he left the room.

HE PATTED HIS FOREHEAD. As far as he could tell, the gash was not bad. The bleeding seemed to have stopped almost immediately. Indeed, after a moment, he had a hard time telling where exactly the gash itself was.

He pulled himself up to sit, still feeling pain deep within each movement, and straightened his legs as best he could. Then he lay back again and began to think.

What did he know? Very little. He had been stored—he knew that somehow, knew what that meant, but could not for some reason remember where he had been stored or why. Nor why they, whoever *they* were, had unthawed him. He knew his name, Horkai, or at least a name that sounded plausibly like it could be his own. He knew, looking at his arms, that for some reason his skin was exceptionally pale. He knew, looking at his body and running his hand over his head, that he was hairless, and remembered, or thought he remembered, losing his hair in a blast. There was a name for it, for the blast, or for the thing the blast had been part of, something he could remember: Kollaps. Why had that come to him seemingly more naturally than his own name? He could remember something about the Kollaps itself but very little about what he had done before or what he had done after, in the days just before being stored.

How long had he been stored? Was his brain sufficiently awake now that he could trust it? He closed his eyes, trying to capture and organize the bits and scraps that beat around his skull.

And why hadn't he remembered he was a paraplegic?

Even if his mind hadn't remembered it, wouldn't his body still have known? Wouldn't it have done something to prevent him from throwing himself off the table?

He patted his leg, but couldn't feel anything in it. He tried to move it, failed. Why, now that he'd been told he was paralyzed, didn't it feel right? Was he in denial?

The problem, he began to realize, wasn't just trying to assemble the little he thought he knew into a narrative—it came in determining which of the memories were real, which were things he'd dreamed or imagined.

3

HE MUST HAVE FALLEN ASLEEP, must have dozed off again. The next thing he was conscious of was the sound of male voices, the feel of their hands as they lifted him off the floor. He saw three of them, one holding his legs and one lifting each side of his body. Or, rather, four: the original technician had returned as well, though he kept his distance, standing back by the door.

Horkai winced at their touch, groaned.

"Awake, then?" asked one of them, a ruddy man with a wispy beard and a pockmarked face. He didn't wait for a response.

They balanced him on the edge of the table a moment, muttering back and forth to one another, then gathered him up more securely. The ruddy man came around behind him. He worked his arms under Horkai's arms and locked his hands over Horkai's chest. The other two made a kind of chariot for his hips and legs. They were larger than the ruddy man. One was black haired and the other brown haired, but otherwise they were seemingly identical in appearance: brothers, maybe twins.

"Still getting your bearings?" the ruddy man asked from behind him, his breath warm against Horkai's ear. "Can't imagine what it's like to be frozen for so long. Nor what it's like waking up."

"It's terrible," Horkai said.

"Of course it is," said the ruddy man affably. "But you're awake now," he said. "Oleg, Olaf," he said. "Might as well do this. He's not getting any lighter. Down to the end of the table and off it on the count of three."

Horkai braced himself, but it didn't seem to lessen the pain when they lifted him. The ruddy man's arms felt like they were cutting him in two, each line of contact like a band of fire. *What's wrong with me?* he wondered. *How can I make it stop?*

"Knus, get the door for us, will you?" said the ruddy man, his voice abrupt with effort. "It's the least you can do."

"All right, Rasmus," the technician said, and Horkai watched him pull the door open. The others, grunting, lumbered awkwardly across the room, maneuvering him through the door and out.

Beyond the door was an access hall. It was wide and long, the floor made of concrete that was weathered and cracked. The walls, concrete as well, were falling apart and roughly patched, holes covered with warped half sheets of plywood smeared with tar. The ceiling was also plywood, a series of layered sheets, the gaps filled with something that looked like tinfoil but had a bluish sheen. It was propped up here and there with lengths of pipe, some still gray with grease, others mottled with overlapping ovals of rust.

"Doesn't look much like it used to, does it, Josef?" said Rasmus. "We've done our best to keep things going, but I'm the first to admit it hasn't always been easy."

"We've kept up the important things," said either Olaf or Oleg.

"The things that matter," said the other brother.

"Time, the great destroyer," said the first. And both brothers laughed.

"How long has it been?" asked Horkai.

Rasmus's steps stuttered, and Horkai dipped in the brothers' arms as they tried to compensate, the jostling causing him a fresh burst of pain.

"Knus didn't brief you?" asked Rasmus. "He was supposed to."

Horkai had to wait a moment for the pain to subside before he could respond. "Knus and I had a bit of a misunderstanding," he admitted.

"I heard you tried to kill him," said Oleg or Olaf, raising an eyebrow.

"We all heard that," said Rasmus. He smiled. "Should we be worried, Josef?"

He acted as if he were joking, but there was an undertone in his voice that made Horkai wonder. *But why would they be nervous about me?* he wondered. *I'm paralyzed.*

The hall ended in a sort of garage door painted brick red. The paint had peeled away in places to reveal bare metal. A large hand crank was to one side.

"Olaf, help me hold him," said Rasmus. "Oleg, take care of the door." Rasmus inclined his head to Horkai, gave a tight smile. "Josef, we'll have to go outside. It's not as bad as it was before—not here, anyway—and in any case, we won't be out long. But we'll still have to move quickly. There's no reason to be nervous."

"Why would I be nervous?" asked Horkai.

"Each minute out there is a day we won't live," said Olaf.

"That's the spirit," said Rasmus, but whether to him or to Olaf, Horkai couldn't say.

He might have continued to question them, but at that moment the black-haired brother let go. Olaf grunted and planted his feet, while Rasmus tightened his arms around him and pulled back. Horkai screamed and passed out.

WHEN HE CAME CONSCIOUS AGAIN, it was to hear Olaf say:

"—not so tough now, is he?"

"Looks can be deceiving," Rasmus responded.

Oleg had managed to roll the door up five feet or so. He rolled it up another foot, then turned around. Horkai groaned, as if just regaining consciousness.

"Awake? As time goes on, you'll probably feel less pain," Rasmus said.

"Probably?" Horkai said.

Rasmus smiled. "No promises," he said. "To be honest, we don't know all that much."

"Why not?"

"Door's open, time to go out," said Rasmus. "Action not words, friend. Olaf, you'll have to walk backwards. I'll let you set the pace. Oleg, close up quickly and then catch up with us."

They moved forward and through the opening. Outside was a ravaged landscape, ruin and rubble stretching in every direction, the ground choked in dust or ash. Remnants of buildings, mostly collapsed. The sky was bleak with haze, and a wind blew, hot and indifferent. All of it was pervaded by a strange, unearthly silence. Olaf, Horkai suddenly realized, was holding his breath. Looking up, he saw Rasmus had his mouth closed tight, too. He heard a crunch as the metal door slid down behind them, then Oleg's footsteps as he came rapidly alongside Olaf, helping take Horkai's weight.

They traveled maybe fifty yards, maybe slightly less, Olaf and Oleg moving backwards crablike and quick, Rasmus pushing them forward until they came to a web of metal girders and shattered glass. Beside it, behind a broken stretch of pediment, was a hole and within it a set of granite steps leading down into darkness. It was into this that they took him, down to a thick metal door and through it, down a winding rusted iron stairwell and into the remnants of an old library, mostly a wreck now.

The bottom level was lit by a strange glow, an artificial light of some kind that seemed to emanate from the walls themselves. The light was pale, just enough to see by but little more. He saw a crowd of perhaps two dozen people, all middle-aged, who began to whisper back and forth as they came in. Rasmus nodded to them, but quickly moved past and to a scorched wooden door on the other side of the chamber.

The room inside was the same, the walls aglow, though perhaps more feebly so. It contained a desk with a single chair behind it. Three chairs faced it.

They carefully deposited Horkai in the chair behind the desk, and he spread his palms flat on the desktop to keep from falling. Then they took the three chairs facing him.

"Comfortable?" Rasmus asked. In the dim light, he looked odd, his outline fuzzy, his eyes pooled in darkness and barely visible.

"That's not exactly the word," said Horkai, his discomfort only slowly receding.

Rasmus nodded. He looked to Oleg, then turned to look at Olaf. "Where should I start?" he asked. And then he looked at Horkai. "Knus didn't tell you anything?"

"Who is Knus?"

"The person who woke you up," said Oleg. "The one you tried to kill."

"Can't you keep anything in your head?" said Olaf.

"Now, boys," said Rasmus. "He's been asleep a long time. It'll likely take him a while to find his bearings." He turned to Horkai expectantly.

Horkai started to shake his head, stopped abruptly from the pain. "He just tried to make me guess my name."

"And did you guess it?"

"We didn't exactly get that far," said Horkai. "I don't like guessing games."

Rasmus sighed. "Knus was just following protocol," he said. "He was doing his best to help."

Horkai didn't say anything. Out of the corner of his eye he caught a glimpse of Oleg and Olaf smirking at each other. Or at least he thought it was a smirk; in the low light it was hard to be certain. Meanwhile Rasmus had his fingers tented beneath his chin and, attentive, was staring at him.

"I SUPPOSE YOU'RE WONDERING why we woke you, Josef," he finally said.

"Among other things," said Horkai.

"It's simple," said Oleg. "We need you."

"For what?" asked Horkai.

"All in good time, Oleg," said Rasmus. He turned to Horkai. "Yes," he said, "that's true. We do need you, Josef. But that's hardly where we should begin."

"Do I know you?" asked Horkai.

"Excuse me?" said Rasmus.

"Is that my name? Why do you keep calling me by it?" asked Horkai. "Are we on a first name basis? Do I know you?"

"No," said Rasmus, dragging the word out. "I don't exactly know you. Or rather, I was introduced to you years ago, but I don't exactly remember that. It's something my father told me about. You used to know my father, back when he was in his thirties. He talked about you sometimes. He trusted you."

"What's his name?"

"Lammert," Rasmus said. And when Horkai didn't answer added, "Last name, Visser. He knew you," he said. "He found you."

He turned the name over in his head. *Lammert.* Did the name say something to him? Could he picture a face? No, not exactly, but there was something there, some resonance, a glimmer. "Of course I remember Lammert," he said to Rasmus, not lying exactly, but not exactly telling the truth either. Rasmus nodded, still watching him. "How is he?" Horkai asked.

"Dead," said Rasmus. "But, then again, most people are. He's been dead for a long time, ever since I was a child. He would have been sixty-three this year."

"How long have I been stored?"

"Thirty years. Give or take."

"Thirty years?"

Rasmus nodded. "That's why your memory's faulty and your nerves are off—they haven't been in use for three decades." He looked curiously at Horkai. "How much do you remember about storage?" he asked. "Is that part of your memory hazy, too? Storage isn't meant to be long term, is normally just a few weeks or months, rarely more than a year at most."

"Why would you keep me under for so long?"

Rasmus looked at him strangely. "What do you remember?" he asked.

"Most of it," Horkai lied. Why did he feel compelled to lie?

"Such as?"

"Just begin from the beginning," said Horkai cautiously.

"As you say, I've been stored a long time. It won't hurt me to hear even the parts I already know again."

Rasmus looked at him for a long time, then slowly smiled. "All right," he said. "As you wish." Placing a large hand on each knee, he began to speak.

4

"DO YOU REMEMBER THE REASON you were stored?" Rasmus asked.

Horkai didn't bother to answer. Rasmus swallowed. He seemed nervous somehow. *Why?* wondered Horkai. *What am I failing to understand?*

"Obviously there's something wrong with you," said Olaf.

"Your legs, for instance," said Oleg.

Rasmus nodded. "The legs are a part of it," he said. He licked his lips. "I learned all of this from my father," he said, his eyes flicking momentarily away. "And many years ago at that, when I was very young. If I get some of the details wrong, that's why."

"All right," said Horkai.

"At some point you were exposed," said Rasmus. "I'm not talking about a minor event, about brief ambient exposure like we just went through outside. According to Lammert, you were close enough that the light must have shone right through your skin. Close enough that by all rights you should have died."

"But you didn't die," said Olaf.

"At least not completely," said Oleg.

"Be quiet, you two," said Rasmus. "Let me do the talking." He turned back to Horkai. "What did happen," he said, "was that you lost all your hair, every last bit of it. On the side facing the blaze, your skin was charred to a crisp. And then you lay there. For how many days and nights, who can say? Until someone found you."

"Your father," said Horkai, thinking at the same time, *Did this* really *happen? What* really *happened?*

Rasmus nodded. "Lammert. He thought you were a corpse at first, but you moved. He was sheathed, but still couldn't stay out long if he wanted to stay alive. But there you were, half your body blackened, exposed for days, unconscious, but still alive."

"And then he—," started Oleg.

"Shut up, Oleg," said Rasmus, then turned back to Horkai. "He stood you up and shouldered you and carried you back is what he did. He installed you in a secure ward—we still had such things in those days," he said, turning to Oleg and Olaf. "He attached you to an IV and waited for you to die."

"Only I didn't die," said Horkai.

"Not exactly," said Rasmus. "In a way, you didn't die. In another way, you died over and over again. Your throat would fill with fluid. Your breath was at first sticky and then rattling and then it would stop completely. Sometimes for hours, apparently. And then, minutes later, hours later, seemingly dead, you suddenly would cough up dark clots of blood and start breathing again. It was terrible to watch, my father said. It was like death was toying with you, killing you and then bringing you back again. He used to describe how he watched you, how once he even went so far as to drag your body away to dispose of it, only to find, once he was already well on his way down the hall, that you were no longer dead.

"And then, after days and days of this, weeks of hesitation and fumbling along the border between life and death, something changed in you. It terrified him. Over the course of a few days, your ruined skin sloughed away to reveal unblemished, hairless pink flesh beneath. A day or two later, you opened your eyes and spoke, just as if nothing had happened."

Horkai nodded. "What did you think?" he asked.

"Me?" said Rasmus. "I didn't think anything. I wasn't there. I was just a child."

"What did your father think?" Horkai asked.

"My father was surprised," said Rasmus. His cadence was like that of someone telling a well-rehearsed story. "He thought that at the very least all that exposure should have ruined your mind, that if nothing else, it should have made your brain sizzle in your skull and driven you mad."

"But your mind wasn't affected," said Olaf.

"You were fine," Rasmus admitted. "You seemed to be doing all right." He looked down at his hands. "Had this happened now instead of then, you would have been in trouble. You would have been decapitated or burned. But my father wasn't superstitious."

"There were explanations," said Olaf.

"Science can explain anything," said Oleg.

"Or could," brooded Rasmus. "Nowadays, who knows? Science doesn't really exist anymore, at least not like it used to. It was designed not for this world but the world before it." Rasmus grabbed hold of the chair's arms, straightened up. "Where were we?" he asked. "Oh, yes. In time you seemed fine, okay, as impossible as that was. But even early on there were slight signs, nervous twitches, moments when you stumbled, when you lost feeling in your feet and toes." He looked again at Horkai. "I learned this all secondhand, of course."

"You can't blame him if he has some of the details wrong," said Olaf.

"It's been thirty years, after all," said Oleg.

"Shut up," said Rasmus, turning to them. "You both talk too much." He turned back to Horkai. "Does any of this ring a bell?" he said.

Horkai thought. Did it? No. The past was a blur, hard to make out. But, ever cautious, he nodded.

"I wasn't there," said Rasmus again. "Don't blame me if a few of the details are a little off. And above all, don't blame the messenger," said Rasmus. He licked his lips. "There's one more thing," he said. "You survived a blast that you shouldn't have survived, but you're suffering from a degenerative disease. It started with tingling and numbness in your toes and then progressed to an absence of feeling in your feet. Then you lost control of your feet. Slowly it crept up your legs. Eventually you'll be completely paralyzed, suffering from utter immobility."

"Why was I stored?" he asked.

"For protection," said Oleg.

"To save you," said Olaf quickly.

"That's right," said Rasmus. "We've been storing you, for your own good, to save you from being paralyzed. We've kept you stored, waiting to make some progress toward curing you. Before we thought of storing you, we gave you injections in the spine to slow the progress of the nervous degeneration. It's a necessary process, but also painful."

"Exceptionally painful," said Olaf.

"It couldn't hurt more," said Oleg.

"I'm afraid," said Rasmus, "that for your own good we'll have to give you an injection soon."

Then there was silence, Rasmus waiting, staring expectantly at him.

"You've woken me up because you've found the cure?" asked Horkai.

The two brothers laughed.

"Not exactly," said Rasmus. "I wish we had, Josef. I really do."

"Then why wake me up at all?"

"Because we need you," said Olaf.

"We have a problem," said Oleg.

"There's something we need you to do," said Rasmus.

"What?"

"All in good time," said Rasmus. "But first things first. He reached into his pocket, came out with a syringe. He broke the plastic casing off the needle. "I hate to do this, but it's necessary. Let's get it over with."

BEFORE HE REALLY UNDERSTOOD what was happening, Olaf and Oleg each had him by an arm and had dragged him from the chair to fold him over the desk, pushing his face down flat against it. Rasmus's hand was groping at his back, dragging up his shirt.

He felt a sharp stab of pain in the center of his spine; then Rasmus said, "We're in." A pressure began to build, which translated into flickers of pain running up and down his spine and growing stronger and suddenly bursting in his mind. And then he was screaming, bellowing into the desk's metal top. Crazed with pain, he managed to get his hands under him and pushed off with all his might. The brothers were crying out now, hanging on to him as he was clutching at them to keep from falling, twisting between them. He caught a glimpse of Rasmus, a frightened expression on his face, the syringe hanging in his hand, its needle discolored with blood. He struck out once with his forehead and broke Oleg's nose, then again in the other direction and both brothers

35

collapsed, leaving him with nothing to hold on to. He came down hard and lay writhing on the floor.

IN TIME THE PAIN FADED. He lay there exhausted, panting. Rasmus was pressed against one wall, unhurt, looking down at him but keeping a safe distance. Oleg lay groaning and slumped on the floor, holding his face, blood oozing through the gaps of his fingers. Olaf was unconscious, a dark bruise already starting to show on one side of his face.

"I warned you it would hurt," said Rasmus in the same tone one might use to scold a child.

"Seems like it might have hurt them almost as much as it hurt me," said Horkai, trying to keep the pain out of his voice.

"He's a monster," whined Oleg, his voice muffled through his hand. "We shouldn't have woken him." It was strange for once not having one brother speaking immediately after the other.

"Hush," said Rasmus. "He didn't mean anything by it," he said. "He just didn't know his own strength. It was the pain that did it, not him. Aren't I right, Josef?"

"Probably," said Horkai. He pushed his splayed legs straight, started to drag himself back to the wall.

"There's no reason to be like that," said Rasmus. "We're on your side, Josef."

"And what side is that?"

"The good guys," said Rasmus, and offered his toothiest smile. "We're the good guys."

Olaf was groaning now. His brother crouched over him, shaking him slightly, dribbling blood on him.

"All for the good of the cause," said Rasmus, following his gaze. "Though let's try not to have the same thing happen next injection, hmmm?"

But Horkai didn't answer. He was busy thinking. When he finally did speak, it was to ask, "If I'm really paralyzed from the waist down, why did I feel that in my legs?"

Rasmus just held his gaze. "You didn't," he claimed at last. "You just think you did."

5

YOU DIDN'T. YOU JUST THINK *you did.*

They had left him alone in a room with a bed and little else. He was lying there in the dim light, trying but failing to fall asleep. *You didn't. You just think you did.* Either Rasmus was telling the truth or he was lying. But he didn't know Rasmus well enough to be able to read him properly.

If he was lying, it meant that he, Horkai, had actually felt something, that there was some feeling left somewhere in his legs. That might mean the nerves could be repaired, that there was hope he might regain his ability to walk. Or it might simply mean that though the legs were paralyzed, the paralysis was not as extensive as Rasmus had been led to believe, that Rasmus wasn't so much lying as simply unaware. Which wasn't to say that Horkai's immobility wasn't progressing, that he wouldn't lose, as Rasmus said, more and more feeling and finally become completely paralyzed. Only that it hadn't progressed as far as Rasmus believed.

So, one hopeful and one not-so-hopeful possibility. But if Rasmus was right and he hadn't felt anything, though, it was more discouraging. It meant he couldn't trust his own senses, couldn't trust what he was feeling and, by extension, couldn't trust what was going on in his own mind. The mind is a great deceiver. He might be experiencing a feeling that was real and he might not be—how exactly was he to know? Which ultimately made him wonder if the whole of his reality wasn't suspect. Was there anything he could know for certain?

Perhaps I'm still in storage, he couldn't stop himself from thinking. *Perhaps something has gone wrong and I've begun to thaw and I'm dreaming. Perhaps this is all a dream.*

He pushed his thumb against his leg. He felt nothing in the leg itself, only in the thumb. He pinched the skin hard, and then harder still, until the skin was broken and the cut began to seep blood. Still nothing. And so he lay there, staring up at the ceiling, trying to find some reason to believe that the world exists.

BEFORE THAT, DIRECTLY AFTER THE INJECTION, he was with Rasmus, propped up again on his chair as if nothing had happened. Olaf and Oleg had left, doubtless to seek medical attention. His spine, where the needle had gone in, still throbbed slightly. It was not painful now, more a dull ache.

"Are you wondering why you're here?" asked Rasmus.

"No," said Horkai, still irritated. "I don't much care. You're the one who woke me. Tell me why or put me back in storage."

A flicker of irritation passed over Rasmus's face but was quickly smoothed over, hidden. "Of course," he said. "Josef, there's something we need that only you can give."

"And what might that be?"

"Something's been stolen from us. A cylinder. We need you to find it and bring it back."

"Why me?"

"Why you? Because of what you used to be."

"And what, in your estimation, was I?"

"You don't remember?" said Rasmus, and shook his head. "Maybe it was a mistake to wake you after all. You were once a fixer," he said.

"A fixer," said Horkai.

"Doesn't ring a bell? It means just what it says," said Rasmus. "You were called upon when nobody else could solve a problem. You were willing to use any means necessary to make things right."

Horkai waited for the words to sink in, hoping for memories to return to his mind. But nothing came. "No," he said. "It doesn't sound quite right."

"I only know what my father told me," said Rasmus quickly. "But why would he lie? You were a fixer, a detective of sorts. You are our last resort. The choice is yours: Either you can lend us a hand for a few days or we can put you back in storage. But if you don't help us, the chances are good there won't be anyone left to get you out of storage later on. We're the ones who can keep you alive, and we're the ones trying to find your cure. Do you want to risk losing us?"

"I'm listening," said Horkai.

Rasmus smiled. "That's all I can ask," he said. He opened one of the side drawers of the desk, removed a rolled piece of canvas. He unfurled it, spreading it on the desk to reveal a crude map.

"This is us," he said, pointing at a black circle, the word *ovo* written over it. "We're all that's left of what used to be there, our numbers spread through what's still standing of some of the university's research facilities. There's the lake, just to the west, and the mountains, just to the east. You'll follow the mountains north about thirty-eight miles, through the ruined towns, and pursue the remains of the freeway across what they used to call the Point of the Mountain. You'll pass the old state penitentiary and then, near the bottom of the slope, the remnants of the highway. Take that up the canyon eight miles or so, and you'll find it."

"Find what?"

"The place where they keep the cylinder."

"How will I recognize it?"

"The cylinder? Red letters on the side. It'll almost certainly be kept in a subzero environment. At least let's hope so. It's no use to us if it isn't."

"No, the place, I mean."

Rasmus grinned, showing the tips of his teeth. "You'll recognize it because of the huge hole bored in the side of the mountain."

"And how do I get in?"

"They don't know you," said Rasmus. "The rest of us they've seen. But you, you can pass, they'll be willing to let you get close. They may even invite you in. After that, you'll have to improvise."

"What do you mean, improvise?"

Rasmus scratched the back of his skull, shrugged. "People have been murdered," he said. "That's what you risk," he said.

Horkai nodded. "And once I get there, I just find this cylinder and take it?"

"You're the fixer, Josef. Figure out how to make things right by any means necessary. Kill them if you have to. Kill them before they kill you. The cylinder is important, much more important than a life or two. Particularly if the lives in question are theirs."

"There's something you're not telling me," said Horkai. "Why did they take the cylinder?"

"I've told you everything we know," said Rasmus.

After a long moment, Horkai said, "Another question." He thumped one of his legs with his fist. "How am I to get there? I can't walk?"

Rasmus shook his head. "You'll be taken there," he said.

"What's in this cylinder?" asked Horkai.

"It doesn't matter," said Rasmus.

Horkai shook his head. "I won't go after it unless I know."

Rasmus hesitated for a long time. "Seed," he finally said.

"What kind of seed. Wheat or something?"

"Yes, basically."

"What makes it special?"

"It's special because it's been kept safe since before the Kollaps. It's undamaged. We need it to start over."

Horkai nodded. "Who'd they kill?"

"These people are ruthless," Rasmus claimed. "When we had the cylinder, we had two technicians working on it. They were tied up and killed, their throats cut from ear to ear."

"And you want me to find out who among them killed the technicians and bring them to justice?"

"That's not what this is about," said Rasmus, waving one hand. "Their deaths are something we have to live with. We don't need revenge. What we need is the cylinder."

No, thought Horkai, *there's still something wrong. Why would grain be kept in a subzero environment? It doesn't make any sense.*

Or maybe that was a method of storage, a way of preserving it that he simply wasn't aware of? Hadn't he heard stories of wheat grown from seeds found in the stomach of a man frozen in a glacier? Why did details like that come back to him and not the important things? Maybe there was a reason for freezing it, maybe even a reason Rasmus himself wasn't sure about.

In any case, the choice was clear. Either he could go

along with it and try to figure it out himself or he could simply go back into storage, to the nonlife he'd been living for the last thirty years. What other choice was there? Illness or no, he didn't particularly want to be frozen again.

"All right," he said. "I'm in."

Rasmus smiled. "I thought you'd see it our way. Get some rest. You'll leave in the morning."

PART TWO

6

MORNING AND AWAKE AGAIN and after a moment of panic relieved
to find he was still himself, still able to remember his name.
Horkai, Josef. His doubts, his nightmares, held at a distance,
at least for now.

He lay on the narrow bed, staring at the bare and glowing concrete walls crumbling in places to reveal a network
of dark rebar. What had the room been before? A large supply closet, maybe, or a small office. What time was it? In the
artificial light, it was impossible to tell. He reached over and
ran his finger along the wall; when it returned, it had picked
up some of the luminescence. Some sort of phosphorescent
bacteria or mold.

He pulled himself to sitting, then forced his dangling legs
to hang off the side of the bed. There was, beside his bed, a
kind of makeshift desk: a metal shelf attached to the wall at
hip level, a chair slid beneath it. He sidled down the bed until
he was closer to it, could make out in the poor light a pad of
paper and a dark stick, perhaps a pencil. There was nothing
else in the room, not a single book.

After moving to the very end of the bed, he found he

could reach out far enough to grasp the door handle, which proved to be locked. *Am I a prisoner?* he wondered. Perhaps he had locked it himself when he reached for it; he looked for a button or some other device on the knob, but no, it was locked, and locked from the outside.

Fair enough, he told himself. He'd nearly killed the technician, almost without thinking about it. He'd sent both Olaf and Oleg to the infirmary. There was no need to read anything into it. Perhaps they were just being cautious.

He scooted back along the bed until he could reach the chair, pulled it next to the bed, heaved his way onto it. He could feel the jolt in his back and spine, but it wasn't the same intense pain he'd been feeling before. His body was already adapting, learning to dampen out and process sensation, blot out pain. Soon he'd be more or less himself again, more or less human. And then maybe his memory would come back as well.

Moving the chair over to the desk proved much harder. Without functioning legs, he had no way to scoot it along. At first he could push against the side of the bed and slide the chair away, but soon he was too far away to get any leverage and his own weight kept the chair from actually moving. In the end, he had to fall out of the chair and then drag it and himself along to the desk and then pull himself up into it.

By the time he was sitting in the chair again, he'd bent one edge of the desk-shelf and cut his forearm. He felt exhausted. How would it be possible to travel forty-six miles like this, even with help? he wondered. Without legs, how could they expect him to go anywhere?

What he'd thought was a pencil was a pen. He toyed with it, twirling it between his thumb and forefinger, and then lined up the pad of paper and wrote. The lines of ink, when they came out, glowed softly:

What I Know
1. I was stored for thirty years.
2. I have been woken up to perform a task.
3. Something is wrong with my memory.

He stopped, then with his thumb brushed over the words "with my memory" until they blurred and became a glowing splotch. *Something is wrong.* He stared at the wall in front of him. With his memory certainly, but it was more than just that: there was something wrong with the world at large, and something wrong here as well. The locked door suggested as much. He stared at the wall and tried to see, on it or through it, something—some scene, image at least—from his past.

At first nothing came. He closed his eyes, sighed. And then an image flitted through his half-dozing imagination that made no sense at all. He caught a glimpse, as if he were standing inside it, of a dome supported by pendentives, rising over a large rectangular space. It was made of stone, probably granite, and lit only from outside, by small slotted windows high in the dome itself. He could hear a sound like muffled laughter but when he turned toward it, it stopped, starting again once he turned back to the dome itself. The pillars, he saw, were moist, covered in a viscid gray substance that glistened where the sunlight struck it. There were paths of the same substance in the dome above as well, he saw, like snail paths, and there, at the very top of the dome, a rubbery agglutination the length and thickness of his forearm that, suddenly, moved.

He opened his eyes, shook his head. *Probably just fragments of a dream,* he thought, *no reason to think it was a memory.* It didn't make any sense as a memory.

When he looked down, he saw his hand had been busy with the pen and had gone on doodling without him. On the pad below his list were several glowing sets of legs, independent of any bodies, each one carefully circled.

HE HAD TRIED TO BRING the image back, but it wouldn't come, at least not with the vividness or clarity it had come the first time.

He must have dozed off in the chair for a while, for the next thing he knew, he was startled awake by the sound of the door opening. It was Olaf and Oleg. They both looked resentful. A large bruise had spread over the right side of Olaf's face, and Oleg's nose was taped, both eyes blackened and bloodshot.

"He's awake already," said Olaf.

"Probably not too eager to sleep after being stored so long," said Oleg, and smirked.

"What do you want?" said Horkai.

"We want you," said Oleg.

"Time to go," said Olaf.

And then they were taking hold of either side of his chair, starting to lift it up. Olaf was, anyway, nearly tipping him out of it—Oleg had turned to the desk and was looking at the paper.

"What's this?" he asked.

"That's nothing," said Horkai.

"If it's nothing, you won't mind if he takes it," said Olaf as Oleg tore the sheet off the pad and folded it up, put it in his pocket.

He opened his mouth to protest and then thought, *What does it matter?* Without objection, he allowed them to carry him out.

RASMUS WAS WAITING FOR THEM, standing beside his desk, hands clasped behind his back.

"You didn't have to bring the chair," he said.

"He was already awake," said Olaf.

"And in the chair," said Oleg.

Rasmus shrugged. "Put him down over there," he said brusquely, "and go fetch the mules."

"Mules?" said Horkai.

"Hmmm?" said Rasmus, half distracted. "Oh, yes," he said. "Good morning, by the way. Mules. They'll take you there."

"Two of them?"

"You'll ride one and then you'll ride the other."

He thought again of how difficult it had been to get from the bed to the chair. How would he manage to get from one animal to the other?

"Will they have a handler?" he asked. "A, what's the word, a drover?"

Rasmus looked confused. "A what? What's a drover, and why would you need one?"

"Will I be at least given a map? Look at me," said Horkai. "I'm a paraplegic. How am I to control two animals?"

Rasmus face broke into a grin. He threw his head back, burst out laughing.

"What?" said Horkai.

"You think I mean mules like horses," he said. "You really can't remember anything, can you?"

"What do you mean?"

"There aren't any animals anymore. Most were killed in the Kollaps, or eaten shortly after. The few that survived went extinct decades ago. Most of us have never even seen an animal."

"But you said mules," insisted Horkai.

"The mules I was talking about have two legs instead of four. They look human enough. They've been trained to carry you."

"What, for forty-two miles?"

"More like forty-six. Two individuals, actually, taking turns, day and night. The roads are too ruined to do otherwise. They've been trained for it. It's all arranged."

The door opened and he turned toward it. "Ah," he said, "we were just talking about you. Let me introduce you to Horkai, your burden."

ONE OF THE MULES was named Qanik, the other Qatik; they told him to refer to them as the Qs. Both spoke awkwardly, as if waiting for the words to blunder up their throats and into their mouths. Both had dark hair and olive skin but also piercing blue eyes. Both stood well over six feet tall. They were broad shouldered and muscle-bound, identical in appearance as far as he could tell.

"This is your burden," Rasmus told them, speaking slowly and carefully. "You shall deliver him as agreed, and then you shall bring him back safely. That is your purpose."

The mules nodded. "We shall deliver him and we shall bring him back," one of them said. "Or we shall die trying."

The other turned to him. "Hello, burden," he said.

"My name is Horkai," said Horkai.

They seemed confused by that, turned to Rasmus for instruction.

"You may call him Horkai," Rasmus said.

"Burden Horkai," said one of the Qs.

"Just Horkai," said the other.

"Yes," said Rasmus. "Now take him to prepare for your journey."

LIKE OLAF AND OLEG, the Qs seemed brothers, identical twins, but when Horkai asked Qanik about it, he just shrugged.

"We don't have parents exactly," Qanik said. "If you don't have parents, how can you be brothers?"

"But I was first," Qatik quickly added. "Of the two of us, I mean."

"What do you mean, you don't have parents?" asked Horkai. "Your parents are dead?"

But Qanik only shrugged. "We just know what they've told us," he said.

Strange, thought Horkai. And then wondered yet again if what he was experiencing was real or if he was dreaming.

The Qs not only looked alike—they also made almost identical, perhaps exactly identical, gestures. They even had the same facial tic, a slight quiver to their chin just before they spoke. He watched them for a while, moving around the supply room, each going for the same object at the same time. Finally, he couldn't help but ask them if they were real.

"What do you mean, real?" asked one of the Qs, maybe Qatik.

"Of course we're real," said the other, offended. "We're as real as you are."

Which didn't exactly answer his question, at least not in a way he was comfortable with.

WHEN THEY HAD A PILE of objects gathered, one of the Qs picked him up, effortlessly it seemed, and carried him over, seating him against the wall next to it. The other mule handed him a stainless-steel pistol, an old and well-greased semiautomatic.

"It's a Mamba," the Q said. "Or something like it. Probably isn't really that old, just modeled after it. God knows where half the stuff around here comes from. Works basically like a Browning. Know how to use one?" he asked.

Horkai shook his head, but his hands were already breaking the magazine out as if they knew what to do. It was full, fifteen bullets in the magazine and one in the chamber.

The other Q nodded. "You know your way around it," he said. "You'll do fine."

The first said, "That's all the bullets we have, so be careful with them."

"Which one are you?" asked Horkai. "Qatik?"

"*I'm* Qatik," said the other Q, and Horkai looked desperately for marks that would distinguish them. There was nothing he could see. "Now, remember, it's not enough to shoot them."

"Who's them?" he asked.

The Qs exchanged glances. "You can start by shooting them," said Qatik, "but that won't be enough."

"Why not?"

Qatik shrugged. "They're resilient," he said.

"But you know that already," said Qanik.

"What do I know?"

"Being resilient yourself, I mean," said Qanik.

Qatik brought one big hand down on Horkai's shoulder, making him wince. "You'll pick it up," he said. "You'll do fine."

THE GUNS THAT QATIK AND QANIK took were bigger. "But it doesn't really matter," Qanik told him. "They will never let us get close enough to use them."

"Besides," said Qatik, "we won't be at our best by the time we arrive."

Horkai wondered what that meant, but thought it better not to ask. Any answer the Qs would give, he was sure, was more likely to confuse the issue than clarify it.

They took packs, stuffed these with food packets and a series of small metal cylinders filled with distilled water.

"We'll take one pack halfway," said Qanik. "Leave it there for the way back."

"But won't someone steal it?" asked Horkai.

The Qs just laughed. "Have you forgotten what it's like out there?" asked Qatik.

THEY STOOD IN THE SUPPLY ROOM, searching through the packs, counting the food packets, taking a few out, putting a few more in, checking and rechecking their guns and ammunition, until at last they were smiling.

The Qs started to climb into bulky, black full-body suits. The fabric was shiny and far from flexible, and the zippers were further covered by Velcroed flaps. *Radiopaque,* Horkai guessed they were. The Qs carefully checked each other's suits to make sure that there were no openings, no gaps, then donned the hoods and affixed them with seam sealant. The front of the hood was a tempered glass faceplate, a heavily filtered breathing apparatus embedded beneath it, and a small speaker.

"Ready," they said, their voices muffled and lifeless through the speakers.

"What about me?" asked Horkai.

One of the Qs—now that they were in their suits and had been moving around, he'd lost track again of which was which—shook his head. "You don't need one," he said.

"You're not like us," said the other.

. . .

IT TOOK A WHILE for the Qs to figure out how to get him onto the shoulders of one of them and keep him there. But when they tried to leave the supply room, they realized they were far too tall for the door, so had to take him down, carry him like a baby instead. As they set off, walking from the storage room through the common room, Rasmus stopped them.

"Can't go yet," he said to Horkai. "You haven't had your shot."

And so it was off to Rasmus's office, where he found himself pushed down against the desk again, held down this time by two figures in shiny black hazard suits. He heard Rasmus rustling behind him and felt the sudden jab of the needle, the terrible surge of pain. He tried this time not to fight it, not to strike out, and as a result convulsed only a little.

"A big one," Rasmus admitted. "Should last you for a while."

He reappeared, his hands bloody.

The Qs let go of his arms and left him there a moment, lying panting on the desk, until he motioned to them that he was all right. Then one of them picked him up, cradling him like a baby again.

There had to be a ceremony before they set off. Rasmus gave a speech to the community about how here was Horkai, the one who had promised to help, promised to save them. Everyone listened in silence, as if politely. Horkai didn't see Oleg and Olaf, wondered distractedly what had happened to them. He thought about asking Rasmus about them, but there was never a free moment. "Our hope, Josef," said Rasmus, turning to him, "nay, our very lives, are in your hands." There was a halfhearted smattering of applause. Horkai did his best to smile, gave a feeble half wave. And then Rasmus led Horkai and his companions up the stairs to the outer door. The rest of the community trailed along up the steps behind him but stopped well shy of the metal door. At Rasmus's prompting, they all shook hands, and then Horkai and his two companions opened the door, climbed the granite steps, and went out into the waste.

7

A HOT VICIOUS WIND AROSE almost immediately. The sun was out, low to the east, just cresting the mountains, but the air was so hazy with dust that it appeared only as a yellow smear in a filthy sky. A scattering of cockroaches preceded them, scuttling around the mules' feet and out of their way, the only other living things immediately visible in the landscape.

They quickly crossed what had once been a walkway, the concrete now cracked and broken. There were traces of other intersecting walkways, with patches of gouged dirt in between that could've once been lawn. Craning his neck to look behind, back near the opening they had come out of, he saw a large, shattered glass roof, twisted bits of metal jutting out of it, the air here dry enough that despite the time that had passed, the metal had hardly begun to rust.

Almost immediately they passed two additional shattered glass structures, much smaller and set near the ground, then two more. They were hardly bigger than a small house, and low enough that when his mule passed close to the last one, he could look down through it. In the dull glow of the sun-smear, he caught glimpses of rows of shelves, scattered and tumbled, rickety piles of books. He glimpsed as well several dead bodies, some nearly perfectly preserved, others little more than scattered bones. They'd probably been left undisturbed, he suddenly realized, for several decades.

The mule he was riding noticed him leaning and looking, and half turned so that Horkai could see a sliver of his faceplate and, through that, a sliver of his face. "Too bad they chose glass," the speaker on the suit said. "If they had kept it concrete, there would be a lot more safe space. A few more would be alive."

A line of twisted, blackened stumps, too small to be trees—the desiccated, petrified remains of bushes, maybe. More cracked concrete, steps this time, and sufficiently shattered that the mules had to pick their way up them for a moment on all fours. Despite this, the mule beneath him seemed to carry him effortlessly, as if this movement was well practiced. The other was carrying both packs, one slung over his back, the other over his chest, which made him look like he had a carapace.

There, to the east, over the remnants of buildings and through the haze, he could discern the vague shape of the mountains, closer than he'd imagined. He was, he realized, looking for something. And then he saw it, a grayish shape, halfway up the slope. It used to be a letter, he remembered, made of stones arranged on the side of the mountain, several hundred feet tall. What was it again? He couldn't remember. Now it was nearly faded away, lost among the stone of a slope now mostly bare. The slope hadn't always been like that, he sensed, had once been thick with trees and brush, but what had the letter been?

At the top of the stairs, a devastated and semi-collapsed building, roughly in the shape of an X. In front of it, fallen to one side and staring up into the sky, a bronze statue, roughly the same height as his mules. It depicted a man with long hair, clean-shaven and sporting a cravat. He was wearing the bronze equivalent of a heavy old-fashioned coat, a waistcoat beneath, something running over it—the chain of a watch or the strap of a gun holster or the thong of a canteen. In one hand he held a cane, broken halfway down.

The two mules stopped and knelt before the statue. They reached out to touch the statue's forehead, muttering something in unison.

"What is it?" Horkai asked. "Who is he?"

"The founder," said the mule he was riding. He gestured all around him. "He made all this," he said. "The place that this is. Before it was destroyed."

"Is he a kind of god to you?" asked Horkai, suddenly nervous.

"Not a kind of god," said the mule. "The founder. He's not a god. He's not perfect."

"He shouldn't have made these roofs in glass," said the other mule.

"He did the best he could," said the first mule.

"Why do you touch him? For luck?"

The first mule shook his head. "Because this is as far as we've ever gone. We've never gone past him."

"You're kidding," said Horkai.

"No," said the mule. "I am not kidding."

"We came into being there," said the other mule, gesturing behind them. "We have stayed there ever since, studying the maps, waiting for this day. We thank you for making this day possible."

"You're welcome," said Horkai, not knowing what else to say, as the two mules regained their footing and set off again.

8

THEY SKIRTED THE RUINED BUILDING, entered a broken expanse of asphalt, the remains of a parking lot dotted with cars, their tires cracked and mostly gone. Some were ruined and at angles, some parked in an orderly fashion, all of them stripped to bare metal by wind and dust, their windshields often blasted opaque. For a moment, a brief flash, he saw the lot as it had been, surrounded by trees, the curving pedestrian bridge leading a few hundred feet or so away to a stadium or coliseum, and then the vision was gone.

The bridge to the stadium was collapsed now, and the stadium, too, must have fallen, was no longer looming visibly over the road. In the lot, most of the cars were empty, though in a few he thought he saw bodies curled on the seats, long dead. Some cars had their doors open and here and there, where the asphalt was most intact, he saw odd dark stains. Distorted shapes, not unlike human bodies.

They approached a corner of the lot, beyond which remains of streets ran to the four points of the compass. At the edge of the lot they paused, and the mule walking beside him turned to him. "Does this look familiar?" the mule asked.

"Some of it," Horkai admitted.

"Can you help us know where to go next?" the mule asked.

"I don't know," he said. "I'll try."

He looked out across the intersection, to where on the far side the hill descended into a field of rubble. He tried to remember what had been there. Dormitories, maybe. To his left side a slope upward, with whatever was behind it hidden. To the right it sloped downward, going first east and then south to reveal the dark scar that the valley below had become, the lake far beyond it, a mottled gray on the horizon.

"Which way?" asked the mule. "We should not waste time."

Horkai raised his hands somewhat helplessly, let them fall. "Straight ahead," he finally said.

The two mules exchanged glances, though because of their hoods, Horkai had difficulty seeing the expressions on their faces. "Straight ahead we go," said the mule beneath him, and they started off.

A SLOW BUT MILD DESCENT, picking their way through the rubble, then, soon after, an open stretch of dirt and dust. The wind picked up and blew dust everywhere. He began to wish he were wearing a suit himself. He squinted, ended up pulling his shirt high to cover his mouth, his nose. They passed an old track-and-field facility, with half-collapsed bleachers, and passed around another stadium just north of it, this one larger and in better condition. The mules gave it a wide berth.

"Why are you avoiding it?" asked Horkai.

"It might be someone's home," said the mule he was riding. "It will only slow us down to have to kill them."

A ruined motel, the remains of an old museum, a replica of a dinosaur skeleton collapsing outside it. They kept up a steady pace, the mules showing no signs of flagging. Another parking lot—this one larger and spattered with large shell craters. They crossed it, came on the other side to the largest street they'd seen so far, perhaps four lanes wide or perhaps six—difficult to tell with the state it was in. In his head he saw it as six, but couldn't tell if it was his imagination or a memory. The road was buckled and torn, but more intact than the streets they'd seen before. On one corner were the remains of a pole and the metal blade of a street sign, but it had been scoured by sand or dust until it was bare metal. *Nothing Road,* thought Horkai. *As good a name as any.* Once they were on it, they moved more quickly.

"It looks promising," said the mule beside him, his voice just audible through the speaker. Either he wasn't speaking directly into the microphone or his speaker had become clogged with dust.

"Which one are you?" Horkai asked.

The mule misstepped but caught himself. He drew a little closer, holding on to the other Q's shoulder, his hand resting softly against Horkai's side. "I'm the older one," he said.

"The first one," said Horkai.

The Q shook his head. "The first of the two of us," he corrected. "But not the first one."

"I'm sorry," said Horkai. "I can't remember the name of the one who was oldest."

"I don't think we told you the name of the one who's the oldest."

"No," said Horkai. "That's not what I mean. The oldest of the two of you. Your name."

"Ah," said the Q. "Why didn't you say so? I'm Qatik."

"Qatik," he said. "Of course you are."

"Why do you say of course? Is it inevitable?"

Horkai shrugged. "I don't know," he said. "It's just a way of speaking. Why were the two of you chosen for this?"

"It is an honor to be chosen," said Qatik.

"Yes, but why?" asked Horkai. "Why you?"

"You are our purpose."

"How did I come to be your purpose?"

"You have always been our purpose," said Qatik.

They moved forward for a time in silence, Qatik still clinging to his brother. Horkai tried again.

"What do you think of Rasmus?"

For a moment Qatik didn't speak. "What do you mean?" he finally said. "He is Rasmus."

"What do you mean by 'He is Rasmus'?" asked Horkai, confused.

"Exactly that," said Qatik. "Rasmus is Rasmus and is no other."

"But that doesn't explain what you think of him," said Horkai. "Do you like him?"

"He is Rasmus," said Qatik. "He has his purpose. How can I judge how well he serves it? His purpose is different from our purpose and I do not understand it nearly as well as I do my own. That is proper. Surely you can see that?"

"Yes, I suppose," said Horkai. "But what does that have to do with whether you like him or not?"

"Exactly. How can I like or dislike someone whose purpose I imperfectly understand? You, however, I can speak about with more authority. You are the burden. As far as I understand that portion of your purpose, you fulfill it admirably. You are sturdy but not overly heavy. You do not struggle when you are carried, you do not scream except when injured, and you do not fall off if you are not tied on. Burden, I like the way you fulfill your purpose."

"Call me Horkai," he said. "And liking the way I fulfill my purpose is not the same as liking me."

"But what are we if we are not our purpose?" asked Qatik. "Burden Horkai, I like the way you fulfill your purpose."

"Just Horkai," said Horkai.

They might have talked more, but Qanik grunted and shrugged Qatik's arm off his shoulder. Qatik fell silent, gradually drifted away. They walked, faster now, Horkai gently rocking up and down as they went.

THE ROAD TOOK THEM SLOWLY UP, edging closer to the mountains—unless it was the mountains that came closer of their own accord.

He thought he saw movement in one of the housing complexes they passed, a series of ruined duplexes that had once been identical and now were collapsed in somewhat disparate ways. Another flat, empty space, perhaps an old sports field. He could see it in his mind, green as it had been, rather than the slightly concave rectangle of dirt it was now. Things were coming back to him, though slowly, and not the important things. Or was it simply his imagination making an educated guess about what had been there?

A huge gouge in the ground 30 feet wide and 150 long, either a long-interrupted construction site or the result of some instrument of devastation. Farther on, in the dust, to one side of an intersection, was a metal signpost, bent over and crushed, the sign itself buried in the dust. Qatik stopped and dragged it up, straightening it until they could see at the end of it the octagonal shape of a stop sign, the word STOP faded but still faintly visible on it.

"What does it say?" asked Qatik.

"Have you never seen a stop sign?" asked Horkai.

Qatik shook his head.

"Can't you read?"

Within his hood, Qatik shook his head again. "Neither of us read. But I can recognize letters."

Beneath him, he felt Qanik nod. "It's not important for everyone to read," said Qanik. "Some read and some do other things. We all have our purpose."

"Who told you that?" asked Horkai. "Someone who can read, I bet."

Not detecting the irony in his tone, Qanik nodded. "Our leader," he said. "Rasmus."

"Should we stop?" asked Qatik. "As the sign instructs?"

"It isn't meant for us," Horkai said. "And besides, we've already stopped. Now we can go on."

Qatik let the sign fall. They walked on, Qanik stopping every once in a while to reposition Horkai on his shoulders. A collapsed strip mall, beside it a building mostly intact. *Probably a bank,* Horkai thought, and then realized that yes that was what it was. He wasn't speculating, he was remembering, this time he was almost certain of it. There were areas that were oddly undamaged—houses with their windows broken out and bricks stripped of paint but otherwise more or less habitable. And then there were other areas that had been all but leveled by mortars or shock waves or dust storms or other weather. Sometimes both areas stood side by side, with a sharp transition dividing one from the other, the whole arrangement artificial and arbitrary enough to make him wonder if it was real.

A Mormon ward house, little left of it beyond a weathered spire and a flattened roof. The houses became sparser, thinning out, and then they thickened momentarily again before thinning out further still.

They came to a large intersection, the road crossing it

almost as big as the one they were traveling, and the mules stopped.

"Which way?" asked Qatik.

Horkai shook his head. "I don't know," he said.

"Which way?" asked Qatik again, as if he hadn't heard. Not knowing what else to do, Horkai pushed on the back of Qanik's head until he moved out into the intersection. From there, he looked to either side. To the east, the road ran quickly south, trailing up a high ridge. To the west, it moved straight ahead, climbing very slowly. In front of them, it continued roughly north, coming still closer to the mountains.

The map Rasmus had given them followed a path between the mountains and the lake. For now, thought Horkai, they would stay close to the mountains and wait for the lake to appear. He pushed on the back of Qanik's head again, and they started forward and through the intersection. Qatik hesitated a moment and then followed as well.

THEY WALKED IN SILENCE for another mile or nearly so, the mountain building up to one side. The wind and dust were making him cough. An old, severely damaged electric substation, transformers crumpled or fallen over in the dust. And then the road split again, one strand of it following a slow curve westward and uphill, toward the lake, the other threading down and into the mouth of a dust-clogged canyon, immediately curving out of sight.

"Which way?" asked Qatik again.

"Maybe the canyon," said Qanik.

"Not the canyon," said Horkai, on impulse.

"Why not?" said Qanik from below him. "The canyon. It goes north, we're going north. We should take the canyon."

"I don't think it goes where we're going," said Horkai.

"Why not?"

"I don't know," said Horkai. "It's just what I feel."

Qatik came around in front of the other mule until their faceplates were nearly touching. They stared at each other for a long time, perhaps moving their lips as well, perhaps even reading each others' lips—it was impossible for Horkai to say, since from above he couldn't see their faces. And then, finally, Qatik backed up, looked at him.

"All right," he said. "We will do as you say."

THEY MOVED ON, the two mules relentless, never stopping to rest. They went up a hill and then hit level ground, crossing again through the remains of neighborhoods, another town, perhaps, or maybe the same one, everything seeming at once familiar and utterly foreign.

They passed an anemic stream, its water bloodred. The mules kept as much distance from it as they could. The sun was high overhead now, perhaps just approaching its apex, perhaps just starting its downward arc. He was thirsty, his mouth dry from the dust in the air, his skin grainy with it and raw from the wind. They passed a ruined school, unless it was something else just as large, maybe a hospital. On the other side was another hospital, unless it was a school. The mules stopped and eyed the latter building for a moment, speaking to each other in muffled voices, their speakers half-covered with their gloves, then shook their heads, continued on.

The road began to slope downward. He could see the lake again now, glowering in the distance two or three or more miles away, looking much larger than it had seemed initially at the other end of town, if they were still in the same town. The water was an odd color, a bloodred tinge to it, though not quite as red as the stream had been. A sort of dead marsh lay beside the lake, sickly gray from this distance. Between them and the marsh, he could see a much larger road: the freeway.

Horkai patted Qanik on the head. "There," he said. "Do you see? That's the freeway. That's what we need."

The mule paused, then nodded. They picked their way toward it, and started north when they finally reached it.

FOR LONG STRETCHES, the freeway was intact and then would suddenly dissolve into a crater or buckle into peaks so that they had to either go around it or clamber up and down it. It took a long slow curve northeast, following the banks of the lake at a distance, and for an hour or two or maybe three, Horkai thought it was the wrong road. Once or twice he almost said something to the mules, but he didn't know exactly what to say, nor did he know what other road they could take. The lake had been on the map, so maybe they were on the right road after all. How many freeways could there be?

And then, at last, the road curved north a little and began to climb. He could see, in the distance, the point where it crested the low side of the mountain, miles away. It was okay, he told himself. It was the right road.

9

BARE LAND ON ONE SIDE, ruins on the other, then ruins on both. It had started to seem all the same to him. "Any chance of a drink?" Horkai asked. "And what about food?"

"Not yet," said Qatik. "Not here."

"My tongue feels like it's made of wool," he said.

"Your tongue is not made of wool," reasoned Qanik. "No tongues are made of wool."

"Soon," said Qatik. "Soon."

What *soon* meant, it was hard to say. They trudged uphill. The sun had slipped lower in the sky. For the first time, Qanik stumbled, almost pitched Horkai off his shoulders. Qatik was immediately there, steadying him. *Shall I take him?* he was saying. *Shall I have my turn?* But Qanik, waving him off, kept going.

And then Qatik took off on his own, running hundreds of feet ahead of them, finally vanishing off the side of the road.

"Where's he gone?" asked Horkai.

"Do not worry," said Qanik from below him. "He will come back."

"I'm not worried," said Horkai. "I just want to know what he's doing."

But Qanik kept walking and didn't respond.

They went a little farther in silence, Qanik grunting occasionally, his steps slightly less steady.

"How many hours have passed?" Horkai finally asked.

"What do you mean, hours?" asked Qanik.

"You don't know what hours are?"

Qanik didn't bother to respond.

"How much time has passed since we started?" asked Horkai.

"Most of the day," said Qanik.

"Can't you be more specific than that?"

"How?"

He was traveling with a man who seemed not to know what hours were.

He had no watch, no way to measure time, nor had he seen anything like a clock at the community. "When night falls, I can be more specific. Then it will be one day."

Something had appeared in the road, perhaps a half mile in front of them, perhaps more. It was moving. Horkai's heart skipped a beat before he realized it must be Qatik.

"Isn't there anything alive out here?" he asked.

"Roaches," said Qanik without hesitation. "Sometimes there are roaches, but only sometimes."

"Anything else?"

Qanik pondered for a long time, his footsteps growing a little less certain. "We are alive and we are out here," he finally said.

"Other than us," said Horkai. "Other than the roaches."

"No," said Qanik. "Nothing can live here."

"Then why can I live here? Why don't I need a suit?"

Horkai felt Qanik's shoulders twitch, wondered if he had forgotten he was carrying Horkai and had tried to shrug.

"You can survive," Qanik said. "That is all I know."

"And how do you know that?"

"Because you are not dead yet."

Qatik loped up, his black suit now covered with white dust.

"I've found a place," he said. "Just off the road, a facility of some kind. Industrial or farming related. A central building, a series of round cylinders as well, ten in all, on supports, with entrances near the base. Some are still standing."

"Anyone living in them?" asked Qanik.

"Not that I could see," said Qatik.

Qanik nodded, gestured the other mule forward with one hand. They followed him up to where the freeway had once crossed over another road—the bridge collapsed now. They clambered down the slope to the roadway below.

What Qatik had called cylinders Horkai recognized as silos. They weren't far, only a few hundred feet from the freeway. The two or three largest had collapsed, caving in on one another, and were little more than bits and pieces of metal ribs now. But many of the others, smaller and perhaps shielded by the larger ones, were more or less intact.

They went toward them, the two mules pointing and nudging each other. They came close to one, walked around it until Qanik pointed to a huge tear in the metal. They moved on to the next one.

"What are you looking for?" asked Horkai, but neither of them answered.

The roof of the next was gone and they passed it by. The next still was slightly larger and they walked completely around it, squeezing their way through the gap between it and the next one. Finally Qatik turned, eyebrows raised.

"It will do," Qanik stated.

With Horkai's help they found the manual hatch release and Qatik tugged on it, but nothing happened. He pulled harder and Horkai heard the metal groan, but it was not until Qanik lumbered forward and grabbed hold as well that the hatch finally sprang open and tens of thousands of husks of long-dead beetles poured out, a fine powdery dust along with it.

When it had stopped, Qatik crunched to the top of the pile and, grabbing the lip of the chute, tried to pull his way in, but the opening was too small. He shucked the two backpacks and this time wriggled in. A moment later, his gloved hand was thrust back out, waited there, palm open.

"Come on," said Qanik, and reached up to lift Horkai off his shoulders. He hung there helpless in the air, his lifeless legs dangling, like a child's doll, and then Qanik thrust him up to the chute opening and Qatik's hand closed around his shirt, dragging him awkwardly in, setting him down roughly on a narrow metal ledge.

"Find something to hold on to," said Qatik, and thrust his hand out again.

There was a ladder beside him and he grabbed it with one hand. His gun was digging into his side so he took it out, balanced it on the ledge beside him. It was extremely hot inside, the air almost unbreathable. It was also very difficult to see. The only light was that coming up through the hatch and from an opening high above, a flap in the top of the roof, where the grain must have in the past been poured in. The backpacks flopped in beside him and then, suddenly, the light dimmed and, grunting, the black-suited form that was

Qanik forced itself through. Once he was all the way in, he turned around and reached back out, pulled the hatch door closed with his fingers.

"Are you sure we'll be able to open it again?" asked Horkai.

"Should be," said Qatik, and then started up the ladder, nearly crushing Horkai's fingers. Down below, beside Horkai, Qanik braced his legs against the inner edge of the hatch chute and dug through one of the backpacks, at last removing a fusee, which he cracked and threw down to rest on the hatch itself. It lay there, burning with a pale red light that cast wavering shadows all through the bottom of the silo. The acrid smoke made Horkai cough. Meanwhile, Qatik had climbed all the way to the top. Leaning far out, he pulled the upper opening closed.

Once he was down, the two mules untaped their hoods, careful to try to preserve the seal for later. They didn't take them off, just slid them back on their heads so that their mouths were visible. Their chins, Horkai saw, were slick with sweat.

"Hungry?" asked Qanik. It was strange to watch someone talk when all you could see of their face was their mouth.

"This isn't a good idea," said Horkai. "The silo is going to fill with smoke."

"We will not stay here long," said Qatik. "We have enough air for what we need."

"We will eat and then we will go," said Qanik. He twisted the end off a metal cylinder and handed it to Horkai, motioned for him to drink. He did—water, warm and with a somewhat metallic taste. Qatik was already handing him a tin box that, when he opened it, he found to be full of hardtack.

"Pour some water into the box and wait a moment," said Qatik. "Otherwise you will break your teeth."

He poured the water in and waited. His eyes were burning from the smoke, making it difficult to see. He felt like he was suffocating.

"You're certain I don't need a suit?" asked Horkai. "You're certain I'll be all right?"

Qanik nodded. "You always have been," he said. "If not, we'd already know."

"How?"

"Skin rash at first, mild in the beginning but getting worse and worse. Then you would start to vomit blood. Around here, it wouldn't take long for your skin to break into sores and ulcerate. If we were exposed to as much as you've been exposed to today, our circulation would be damaged and our hearts would fail."

"Why hasn't that happened to me?"

Qanik shrugged. "You are okay," he said. "You always have been. You are not in any trouble."

"We are the ones that are in trouble," said Qatik.

"That's why you're wearing the suits," said Horkai.

"They are not enough," said Qatik.

"Not enough?"

"No need to talk about it," said Qanik.

"But I want to talk about it," said Horkai.

"You do not want to hear about it," said Qatik.

"Both you be quiet and eat," said Qanik.

Horkai looked at the tin in front of him. The water had softened the hardtack, making it a little more flexible. He took a bite, found it tasteless, but managed to choke it down. He took a sip of water, another bite of the biscuit.

"I want to hear about it," he said, chewing. "I want you to tell me."

"Not a good idea," said Qanik.

"He has a right to know," said Qatik. As he spoke he ate, breaking off a corner of damp hardtack and chewing it. Both the mules, Horkai realized, were eating much more than he was, and eating much quicker.

Qanik shrugged.

Qatik turned to Horkai. Horkai watched his mouth moving just below the edge of the hood, the rest of his face hidden behind the shiny black fabric.

"These suits keep out only so much," said Qatik. "They do not protect us completely."

"So this will damage you?" asked Horkai.

"Not damage," said Qatik. "Kill."

"Kill? Then why are you doing it?"

"We are the mules," said Qanik. "This is our purpose. This is what we were made to do."

"Who told you that?"

"That is how it is," said Qanik.

"But who told you?"

"Rasmus," said Qatik.

Rasmus, thought Horkai. *Always Rasmus.*

"Can't you do something?" he asked them. "Can't you make better suits for yourself? Can't we stop it?"

Qanik shook his head.

"What if we turned back now?"

"We are the mules," said Qanik firmly. "This is what we do."

"But—"

"What Qanik means," said Qatik, interrupting him, "is that we are already dead. We have already been out too long. If we turn back, we still die, just not as quickly."

"Don't you care about that?"

Qanik shrugged. "We all have to die sometime," he said. "Better to die doing what you are meant to do."

"As mules," said Horkai.

"As mules," said Qanik, nodding.

Below them the fusee was sputtering, the shadows leaping more erratically. "Enough talk," said Qatik. "Back in the hood, Qanik. Time to go."

LATER, WALKING AGAIN but riding on Qatik's shoulders this time, moving upslope and coming closer to the point of the mountain, the sun now threatening to set, he tried to raise the issue with them again. At first he tried to ease into it gently, tapping on Qatik's hood to attract his attention.

"If you're going to die anyway," he asked, "why wear suits at all?"

Qatik's response was muffled. Horkai leaned forward and swiveled one ear and then asked him to repeat it.

Qatik tapped his speaker to clear it. "If we did not wear our suits, we would already be dead," he said. "We would not be able to achieve our purpose."

"Why trade your lives for a purpose?" asked Horkai. "What makes that a worthwhile trade?"

Qatik slowed, briefly came to a stop. Qanik, to one side, turned slightly, raised an eyebrow behind the faceplate. "Why are you trying to make me doubt?" Qatik asked. "Why now, when it is already too late, when I am already dead, when my purpose is all that is left to me?"

He started up again, slow at first. Qanik fell into step beside them.

"And what if you convince us?" asked Qatik. "The best that can happen is for us to decide there is no point carrying you and leave you here, on the side of this roadway, to die."

He had, Horkai had to admit, a point. Quickly, he changed the subject.

"If you've never been outside, how do you know what things are?"

"We had been as far as the founder," said Qatik.

"Still," said Horkai. "That's not very far."

"Pictures," said Qatik. "We've been given instruction. We have seen maps. We were given scenarios and made to solve them."

"But it was not always perfect instruction," said Qanik. "You had, for instance, to help us to open the hatch on the cylinder."

"The silo," said Horkai.

"Silo," they said in unison.

"Farming related, then," added Qatik. "We saw many pictures and we memorized many things."

"And among those pictures were images of farms?"

"No," Qatik admitted. "Among those pictures were images of farming-related buildings."

"Do you know what a farm is?"

Qatik didn't respond.

"A farm," said Horkai, "is a stretch of land used to grow agriculture and livestock."

"What is agriculture?" asked Qatik.

"Plants grown for food. You know what plants are."

"There are plants near the founder," said Qanik. "But they are dead. If you touch them, they break and sometimes fall into dust."

"There are no longer living plants," said Qatik. "There are fungus and mushrooms, and that is what we eat. *Agriculture* is no longer an important word. This is why we were not taught it. It is not important we know it. What is livestock?"

"Animals grown for food," said Horkai.

"There are no longer animals," said Qatik. "This is no longer an important word. It serves no purpose."

"How do you know there are no animals?"

"Rasmus told us," said Qatik.

"How does Rasmus know?"

But Qatik refused to answer the question. They walked on in silence awhile.

"Where do your names come from?" Horkai asked. And when Qatik said nothing, he asked again, louder this time, hoping to draw Qanik in.

"They were given to us," said Qanik.

"What do they mean?"

"They do not mean anything," said Qanik. "They are names."

"No," said Horkai. "That's not what I mean. I mean where do they come from? Are they family names? Are they something from your ancestors' culture?"

"I do not know," said Qanik.

"You don't know?"

"He never told us where they came from."

"He? Who's he?" Horkai asked, even though he already knew what the answer would be.

"Rasmus," said Qanik. "Rasmus gave us our names."

"Why would Rasmus name you? You're as old as he is."

"We are not as old as he," said Qanik. "Not nearly. And I, I am not even as old as Qatik."

"Maybe Rasmus gave you your name as well," said Qatik to Horkai. "Are you certain your name is really your name?"

THE SUN HAD SLID BEHIND the western mountains; all that was left of it was a wavery slit, and then that, too, was gone. There was still light but it was gradually fading away and would soon be gone entirely.

Qanik came close, rested his hand on Horkai's lower back. "I can now be more specific," he said. "It has been an entire day."

Horkai nodded. "When do we stop to sleep?" he asked.

"We do not stop to sleep," said Qatik. "There is no time. We stop when we die."

10

BY THE TIME THEY HAD REACHED the place where the freeway skirted the edge of the mountain and started back down, it was so dark that Horkai couldn't see at all. The wind whipped viciously around them, making his shirt flap against his body. It was troubling to be moving through the darkness with no idea where you were going. The mules seemed to have no trouble picking a sure-footed path forward, didn't even bother to slow down. As they passed over the top and started down, the wind tapered off, going suddenly quiet.

Above in the sky, behind the haze, arose a pale blur that he realized must be the moon. It helped him see again—though just a little, just enough to differentiate between the ground and the shape of Qanik walking beside them. If there were buildings to either side of the road, or farms, he couldn't see them. There was a glimmer that might be water or might be something else. Nowhere were there any man-made lights.

For a long time he stayed still, listening. There were no insect noises, no birds, only the measured tread of the mules' footsteps.

"How can you see?" he finally asked Qanik.

"We can see," said Qanik. "That is how we are."

"Maybe after a time, you will be able to see," said Qatik. "Maybe your eyes will adjust."

He waited for them to adjust, but nothing seemed to be happening.

They trudged on. They passed through an area that smelled odd. Not a bad smell exactly, or a dead smell: something else. The mules, he noticed, had sped up, unless he was imagining it.

He watched the moon smear its light through the haze. He tried again to make out the land around him, without success. He rocked back and forth, suspended in darkness. *Just as,* he couldn't help but thinking, *I've been suspended in darkness for the last thirty years, stored. Is this so different?*

And what if, he couldn't stop himself from thinking, *it has all been a dream, a momentary burst of electricity in my brain caused by some small short or malfunction within the storage tank? What if I'm still, even now, in storage?* That would make more sense than this ruined, lifeless world, or the fact that he seemed to have different characteristics from those around him, that he could withstand things that none of the others could. The silo, once he started thinking about it, was a lot like the tank, but very hot instead of cold—perhaps his brain was trying to tell him something. *What if none of it is real?*

And if it is a dream, he wondered, *will it stay a dream or become a nightmare?*

He closed his eyes. *This isn't real,* he told himself. *This isn't real.* But no matter how often he said it, no matter how much he tried to think the world away, he could still hear the sounds of footsteps crunching beneath him, could still feel the rocking rhythm of Qatik's gait.

HORKAI PATTED QATIK'S HEAD gently.

"Doing all right?" he asked.

Below, the mule made a sound that he took for assent.

"Would it help keep you awake to talk?"

After a long pause, Qatik said, "Maybe."

"Tell me about yourself," said Horkai. "Tell me who you are."

"I have already told you," said Qatik. "A mule."

"And the oldest," said Horkai.

"The older of the two of us," said Qatik, "but not the oldest."

"And you have no parents. And despite looking alike, you are not brothers."

"We do not have parents," said Qatik. "We are not brothers."

"Everybody has parents."

He felt Qatik shake his head through the hood. "That is not how we are."

"None of us have parents," said Qanik, coming closer now. "Not in our community."

"But Rasmus does," said Horkai. "He told me the name of his father."

Qanik shook his head. "You misheard. Rasmus is one of us. None of us have parents."

"You've given up your parents?"

"If you like," said Qatik.

"We share everything. All property is held in common," said Qanik in a singsong voice. "We have no parents. Each of us is his own man, and each of us has a part to play in the community. We must accept our purpose or the community shall suffer."

"Rasmus taught you this, I'm guessing," said Horkai.

They didn't respond.

"You're communists," said Horkai.

"What are communists?" asked Qatik.

"We are not that word, whatever it means," said Qatik. "We are a hive."

"A hive?"

"Like a beehive," said Qanik. "It is our symbol. A united order. Next to the welfare of the community, our own welfare is nothing. We each have a part to play and we must play it. We must consecrate our lives to the service of our whole. Each of us has our purpose and each of us must fulfill that purpose or the community shall suffer."

"Sounds almost like a religion," said Horkai.

"A hive," said Qatik again. "A united order. The many as one. No more, no less."

"Who holds the property in common? Who distributes it?" asked Horkai. "Rasmus?"

Qanik didn't respond.

"Don't you think—?" he started to say, but then stopped as below him Qatik came to a halt, stood there motionless. "I agreed it might help to talk," he said. "You asked me and I gave my assent. But now I no longer want to talk. And I no longer want you to talk with Qanik. Not about these things."

Horkai stared down into the darkness, trying to discern him, but made out little more than the feeble outline of his hood. "All right," he said. "We don't have to talk anymore."

He felt Qatik nod once through the hood, and then they moved on.

· · ·

QATIK'S EASY MOTION was making him sleepy. At times he felt himself beginning to fall, beginning to drop off, and once Qatik had to reach up and hold him in place. Finally, when it kept happening, Qatik reached round and pulled him down, held him instead in his arms like a baby.

The suit was cool against his face, the material strange, not like anything he was familiar with. It smelled of dust and stuck gently to his cheek. He lay there, gently rocking with Qatik's motion. Eventually, he fell asleep.

HE DREAMT THAT HE WAS IN the storage tank, just going under, waiting there with the tubes in his mouth and his eyes closed for the storage to begin. He opened his eyes, and a face on the other side of the glass—a technician of some sort, maybe someone he knew—admonished, "Keep your eyes closed. If they stay open, they might be injured." He nodded, closed them again. He could hear, muffled and as if at a distance, the sound of the technician moving around. *When will it happen?* he wondered. He parted his eyelids just slightly and through veiled eyes watched the technician. He was standing there, his back to the machine, looking at something, and when he turned around, his face had on it a look of mixed fear and surprise, and it seemed, for just a moment, to be directed at him.

Horkai scrutinized the face, pretending to keep his eyes closed. Did the face look familiar? Was it someone he knew? Maybe, but in the dream, just as in life, it was hard to be certain of what he did and did not know.

And then suddenly he felt fluid flood into his mouth. His eyes opened wide and there was a hissing sound, incredibly loud, and he watched ice branch over the glass. He tried to close his eyes but they wouldn't close and he couldn't move. He should have been unconscious now, he knew, his existence blacked out, but he was still there, frozen but still *there,* still thinking. *Help me,* he thought. Through the glass he could hear the technician pacing back and forth, back and forth, back and forth.

11

WHEN HE AWOKE, the sun hadn't risen yet but the sky had started to turn light, the haze streaked through with paler shades. He moved and stretched. When Qatik realized he was awake, he stopped, gestured to Qanik. Qanik nodded, quickly took the pack off his chest then the pack off his back, leaving them lying in the dirt. He lifted Horkai onto his shoulders and set off.

"I can tell you how much time has passed," said Qanik. "A night and a day."

"Are we close?" asked Horkai.

"We are getting close," admitted Qanik.

They had left the freeway at some point. Horkai could see it a mile or two behind them, assuming it was the same freeway. They were heading east now, toward the rising sun, toward the mountains.

"How did you know where to turn?"

"We looked for the crater," said Qanik.

"And did you find it?"

Qanik nodded. "And then we turned."

"How did you know it was the right crater?"

"It was described to us. It was sung to us in detail by someone who saw it who was older than we. He was bleeding already when he sung it to us. He sung it to us and then he died."

Sung? he wondered, but decided not to ask.

The road was large, maybe four lanes across, but not as big as the freeway. It was devastated in places, but someone had pulled the rubble off, arranging it in neat piles to one side. This seemed to make the mules nervous. They came to a place where the road curved south again and climbed, and the mules argued about whether they had taken the right road after all. But eventually, after perhaps half a mile, it wound back east again and straightened out.

They passed a ruined mall surrounded by a huge parking lot, now heaped with piles of dust. A doll's head, Horkai saw, had been placed on the top of a stack of rubble beside the road.

"You're sure there's nobody out here?" asked Horkai. But neither mule answered.

Another parking lot and across from it an old hospital, the central building intact. Not only intact, but someone had covered the windows of the ground floor over with sheets of tin. Behind a window on the second floor came a flash of movement.

"I think I—," he started to say, and then felt incredible pain in his chest. Only afterwards, as he was falling, did he realize he'd heard a shot. He hit the ground hard, suddenly couldn't breathe. His vision blurred and dimmed, then came back. He reached down to touch his chest where the bullet had gone in, found the hole as big as his finger, perhaps even bigger. He moved his hand back where he could see it, stared at the blood on his fingers.

Qanik was shouting, bellowing. Horkai raised his head a

little, saw him running in one direction, Qatik in the other. More shots rang out, a little puff of dust rising beside his head. *He's still shooting at me,* he thought. *He's trying to kill me.* He looked at his bloody fingers again and thought, *Maybe he already has.*

Another shot hit him, but since it was in the leg, he couldn't feel it; he knew he had been hit only because he saw the leg jump and then the fabric of his pants go red with blood. *I should try to crawl away,* he thought, but he couldn't move. He let his head fall back. He closed his eyes, heard another shot, then another, and then he lost count.

12

HE COULDN'T MOVE, *couldn't breathe. The world all around him didn't exist, simply wasn't there. The only thing around him was darkness and more darkness, and nothing he could see or feel. He was both there and not there, suspended in a void, his eyes open; he was pretty sure anyway his eyes were open, though he couldn't blink, couldn't manage anything.*

He stayed there unmoving, trying to move his eyes, try-ing to move his fingers, trying to see something. How long have I been like this? *he wondered.* How long will I be like this?

A FIGURE IN A BLACK HAZARD suit was crouching over him, staring at him through a glass faceplate, repeating his name over and over. It took him a moment to realize it was one of the mules. Qanik or Qatik? He wasn't sure. It hurt to breathe, was hard to think.

"He's dead now," said the mule, and for just a moment Horkai thought they were talking about him. "Qatik found him and took care of him. Just one," he said. "Just a rogue living in the hospital. Had made himself a makeshift suit out of all the X-ray aprons he could find, but it was not a very good suit. He probably wouldn't have lasted much longer."

"I'm dead, too," Horkai said to Qanik, his voice very low.

Qanik just laughed. "You do not know how to die," he said. He reached down and started to gather Horkai in his arms.

Horkai felt a tremendous pressure in his chest and screamed, Qatik stopped, and instead he stood, grabbed him by the foot, and began to drag him.

It hurt like hell but was better than being carried somehow. The sound of his head scraping along the ruined asphalt echoed deep within his skull. He imagined a swath of blood unfurling behind him. He tried not to pass out.

And then Qatik was there, too, asking Qanik what was wrong with him, was he crazy?

"I couldn't pick him up," said Qanik. "It was the best I could do."

They argued back and forth, Horkai watching helplessly from below. He was choking on something and coughed and could tell from the taste in his mouth that it was his own blood. And then, without transition, they were bending over him again, solicitous. One of the mules was taking hold of his hands, the other his feet.

"On the count of three," said one of them, the one nearest his head. "One," he said. "Two. Three." And simultaneously they lifted him off the ground.

Pain shot through his body. His chest felt like it was being torn apart, and then he could no longer breathe. His head filled with light and he was gone.

13

HE WAS LYING NAKED on a bare concrete floor in a dim light, staring at a pile of bloody clothes that it took him a moment to recognize as his own. He smelled something familiar. At first he couldn't place it, then realized it was the smell of a cigarette. He flicked his eyes past them, saw the two hazard suits hanging from a hook on a bare concrete wall. He touched his chest where he had been shot, but felt no scar, only a smooth, slightly softer place where the bullet had gone in. He lifted his hand, stared at it, didn't see any blood.

"You are healing still," said a voice, "but you are alive."

He turned his head, saw the two mules sitting at the base of the wall to the other side of him. It was strange to see them out of their suits. They sat there in the exact same way, knees up and hands resting on them, their heads leaning back against the wall. Between them fluttered the flame of a candle. One of them was smoking, a cigarette hanging from the side of his mouth.

"Where did you find that?" asked Horkai.

"The rogue had some," said the mule. "Don't know where he got them. They're old, but not too old. Someone's growing stuff somewhere." He took the cigarette out of the side of his mouth, stared at it. "Not bad," he said. "We saw a video about them but have never tried them. A little harsh, but I can see how you would get used to it."

"You learned about cigarettes, but they didn't teach you what a farm was?"

The mule shrugged. "Apparently there are still cigarettes," he said, holding his up. "There aren't still farms."

"I don't like them," claimed the other. "Filthy habit."

"You're just repeating what you heard in the video," said the mule.

"Which one of you is which?" Horkai asked.

"You still can't tell us apart?" asked the one not smoking.

"Please," he said. "I've been shot."

The mule who had spoken first sighed. "I'm Qatik," he said. "I will let you sort out who that other one is."

"Qanik," said the other one, and waved his cigarette at him.

"You're no fun," said Qatik to him.

"What did you do with the body of the man who shot me?" asked Horkai.

"We left it as a warning," Qatik said, and smirked.

Grunting, Horkai pulled himself up until he was sitting. He stared down at his chest. The hole that had been there was covered with a pliant layer of membrane, thick and semi-transparent.

"What is this?" asked Horkai. "What's on me?"

"Nothing is on you," said Qanik. "That is you."

"What do you mean it's me?"

"Exactly what he says," said Qatik. "You are different. It does not hurt you to be outside, and when you are injured, you heal very quickly."

"It's not natural," said Horkai.

Qatik shrugged. "It is the way you are," he said.

"Why?"

"Ah," said Qanik. "The good old questions. Who am I? Where do I come from? Where am I going?"

"No," said Horkai. "Just one question. Why am I the way I am? Why aren't I dead?"

"This makes two questions," said Qatik.

Horkai didn't respond. He stared at the two mules, who simply stared back. Finally, Qatik shrugged again. "We do not know," he said. He lifted his arm and rolled back his sleeve, then moved it so it was fully lit by the candle. The skin, Horkai saw, was mottled, covered with a sort of red rash, seeping slightly. There were bruises running underneath the skin as well, unless it was simply the way the shadows were cast.

"We, on the other hand," Qatik said, "do not heal quickly."

"WHERE ARE WE?" he asked once he had slipped back into his clothes, which were still stiff with dried blood.

"A shelter below the hospital," said Qanik. "Nice solid concrete walls, very safe here. You can see why the rogue liked it."

"Why do you call him a rogue?"

"Because it was just him," said Qatik. "He is not in a hive."

"If you are not in a hive, you are a rogue," said Qanik. He stubbed out his cigarette on the concrete floor, reducing it to flinders that he then swept away. "If you are not part of a hive, you are nothing."

"According to Rasmus, I imagine," said Horkai.

Qanik nodded. "According to Rasmus," he assented.

"It is safe here," said Qatik again. "We were lucky. We found a nice place to stay and recover. If it had been another hive and they'd been hostile, we would be dead."

"At least Qatik and I would," said Qanik. "You might not be so lucky."

"He did not shoot a hole in our suits," said Qatik. "Instead he tried to shoot you. Our suits are still intact. We might still achieve our purpose."

"But we have no food," said Qanik.

"Yes," admitted Qatik. "That is a problem. Though not as much of a problem as water. We have a little water still, but only because the rogue had some."

"If it is all the same to you," said Qanik, "we'd like to go now."

"All right," said Horkai. "We can go."

HE BEGAN TO MOVE TOWARD THEM by sitting and dragging himself backwards. He was surprised when one of his legs seemed to twitch, though he didn't feel anything. Maybe he was just imagining it, or his body had turned a bit.

He stopped and made a conscious effort to move the leg. It didn't obey his command exactly, didn't rise or change position, but did twitch again.

"Hey," he said, "did you see that?"

"See what?" asked Qatik.

So he scooted around until they could see his legs better, then pointed to the one that had twitched, made it twitch again.

"It's regaining movement," said Horkai.

Qatik shook his head. "Start of a spasm," he said.

"That is another thing," said Qanik. "We were supposed to be gone only two days, three at most. It has been longer than that."

"We weren't told what to do," said Qatik. "We have been sitting here talking about what steps to take to keep the disease from spreading up your spine until you have medication. And we came up with an idea."

He held up a bone saw.

"We should have done this before you woke up," said Qanik. "That was our plan. But it was hard to decide who would hold you and who would saw. And you woke up sooner than we thought."

"Saw what?" said Horkai.

"Your spine," said Qatik.

"You're going to saw through my spine?" asked Horkai, his voice rising.

"This is for your own good," Qanik explained patiently. "To stop the disease from spreading. The disease must not spread."

"No, but—"

"All right, then," interrupted Qanik. "We are in agreement."

"If there was any other way," said Qatik, "we would take it."

"But how do you know that my body won't fight off the disease?" asked Horkai.

"Same way as you," said Qanik. "Rasmus told us."

"But look at me," said Horkai, speaking quickly. "I can be shot through the chest with a bullet, and after a few days I'm just fine. Why would a disease hurt me?"

Qanik shrugged. "Life is mysterious," he said.

"Why don't we just see?" asked Horkai. "Why don't we wait and see if anything happens to me. Maybe I'll be fine."

"We can't wait," said Qanik. "We're out of food. We have to go."

"I don't mean wait like that," said Horkai. "We can leave any time you'd like. All I mean is wait to cut my spine."

"It might be too late by then," said Qanik.

"That's a chance I'm willing to take," Horkai said.

Qanik and Qatik exchanged glances. "We should have done it when he was still asleep," said Qanik. He turned to Horkai. "Understand," he said. "There's nothing to be afraid of. It's just a little bit of pain. We will cut low and your spine will grow back. It will reconnect."

"Let's hope it doesn't grow back quickly enough that we will have to do this again," said Qatik.

"That is not helpful," said Qanik, turning to him. "Remember: if you cannot say something positive, do not say anything at all."

"Look," said Horkai, already anticipating the pain. "I'm begging you. Don't do this."

But the two mules were already standing, Qatik holding the bone saw down by his side, Qanik priming a hypodermic. Horkai began to scoot rapidly away from them.

"Can you hold him down on your own?" asked Qatik.

"Probably," said Qanik. "For that long. Besides," he said, louder this time, "he won't struggle, he knows this is for his own good."

THEY MOVED SLOWLY TOWARD HIM, Qanik flanking him on one side and Qatik on the other. Despite their size they were quick, and Horkai, without legs, knew he had no chance of escaping. But still he kept circling, kept backing away.

And then he kept his eyes focused on Qatik too long and Qanik dived in, knocking him flat. Horkai lashed out and struck him in the shoulder, was surprised to see Qanik immediately start to bleed. And then Qanik had him in a headlock, was forcing him over.

He screamed and tried to arch his back to keep from tipping over, but Qanik was too heavy. Slowly he was being turned over, forced down onto his face.

Soon he was flat against the concrete, still in a headlock, Qanik's knee now pushing hard into his back, his ribs threatening to crack. *Quick!* Qanik was shouting, *Quick!* He felt a hand on his back, dragging up his shirt.

Something pricked into his back and he felt a sudden warmth there, the beginning of a numbness, though not numb enough. The bone saw's blade dug deep and his vision was suddenly gone, reduced to a red haze. He screamed and flopped but Qanik rode him, kept him in place. "Again!" the mule yelled, and Horkai gritted his teeth and held his breath and the pain kept coming on stronger, and he passed out.

14

BY THE TIME HE WOKE UP, Qatik had given him a shot of morphine and the pain had moved from blinding and intense to something merely debilitating. But when Qanik tried to pick him up, it grew immediately blinding again.

"All right," said Qanik. He put him down and leaned back, carefully lighting a cigarette off the candle. He raised it to his mouth and Horkai watched the tip glow orange, slowly fade to red, then gray. He saw that Qanik's face was bruised, his nose broken. He wondered if he had done that. He hoped so. "We'll wait, then," Qanik said.

"If you ever do something like that to me again," Horkai said, "I'll kill you."

"See if you still feel that way in an hour," said Qatik.

And indeed, in another hour the pain had faded enough that Qanik could pick him up and hold him in his arms and Horkai only winced. His back, he found upon reaching behind himself to feel the cut, had already started to heal. A spongy soft material of some sort was growing firmer, stronger by the second.

"Shoulders?" asked Qanik.

"Not yet," said Qatik. "He's not ready for it."

And so the two mules put on their suits again and carefully checked each other's seams. When they were satisfied, Qanik bent down and picked Horkai up. He went out cradled in Qanik's arms.

THEY UNBOLTED THE METAL DOOR and started up the winding metal staircase beyond it. Every step jarred a little, was like a dull throb against the severed end of his spine. They came to another metal door and Qatik opened it. Qanik threaded Horkai and himself through.

They were on the ground floor of the hospital, in a dark and dusty room. The outer doors and windows had been covered with sheets of tin, except for one, which had been crumpled and torn partly free. They forced their way out of it.

Outside, he could see the swath of blood they had made dragging him in. He stretched and looked past Qanik's shoulder. The rogue's body had been nailed by the elbows and the knees to the hospital façade. The forearms and lower legs had been cut off, left crossed as a warning to either side of the piece of tin they had just pushed past. The head was nowhere to be seen. What remained of the torso was so thick with dust that he barely recognized it as once human.

"Was that really necessary?" asked Horkai.

Qatik shrugged. "It could have been," he said.

"It could have been worse," said Qanik. "If you had been unconscious much longer, we probably would have had to eat him."

They moved along in silence. Remains of houses now, those that still stood, more or less, were larger than the houses they had seen before, or seemed so to him. Mostly, but not exclusively brick. The road itself was straight, climbing very slightly, the mountains getting closer. They were heading, he could see, for a gap between them. They passed a metal pole still standing, a large rectangular sign on it. One side was stripped bare, but the other side, he saw over his shoulder, was, through some strange fluke of nature, faded but more or less intact. He had to squint to make out what was left of the letters. ERLING D it read, and below that, in smaller script, *00 E.*

"What happened to his head?" Horkai finally asked.

Beside him, Qatik patted one of his backpacks. "Never know when you'll need a good head," he claimed.

THEY PASSED AROUND A SCHOOL BUS that had been turned over on its side and burned. The road grew briefly disjointed and broken and they had to pick their path carefully. The sun, Horkai noticed, was high in the sky, nearly directly overhead. The road here was edged on both sides by a long stone wall, mostly blown out, but the ghost of it still there. The mules plodded implacably forward, saying nothing.

A half-collapsed supermarket, complete with a sign reading ERTS. A scattering of bones around it, blankets of dust as well that might hide more. More parking lots, more malls and shopping centers. The ruins of commerce. A nondescript building that he somehow felt must have once been a coffee shop. Was it a memory?

More ruined walls, the mountains closer now. The road curved very slightly, heading for the mouth of a canyon still several miles ahead. The mules were getting nervous, he realized.

"I'm going to put you on my shoulders now," said Qanik. "So as to have my hands free. All right?"

"All right," said Horkai. And without another word, Qanik swung him around and dropped him there. Pain shot briefly up through his back but was quickly gone. His spine no longer pulsed with each step. He reached back to feel the cut, had difficulty locating it.

What am I exactly? he wondered.

A city bus had crashed decades before into a small building set off the road. The road was still curving ever so slightly. Suddenly it rose a little steeper, curving the other way, skirting around a hill. Houses sparser, a little more spread out now, a little more rural, the road devolving into a simple two-lane highway. An old split-rail fence, somehow in better shape than the stone walls had been. The road winding more now, moving slowly through clumps of long-dead trees, little more than stumps.

Past a small road with a sign scrubbed down to bare metal but upon which someone had written something, relatively recently, in black paint. The dust covering it made it illegible. Qatik left their side and hurried toward it, wiping the dust away with his black glove.

GLACIER LN, it read, the letters thick and clumsy.

"That first letter is a *G*," said Qatik.

"What does it say?" Qanik asked, and Horkai read the sign aloud.

"We're getting closer," claimed Qanik from below him.

They kept on, Qatik rejoining them. A few hundred feet farther along, on the other side of the road, another smaller road split off. There was no metal sign, but someone had put up a wooden post, nailing a placard on it. OLD WASATCH BULLEVARD, it read, the last word misspelled.

"Who is doing it?" asked Horkai, gesturing at the sign.

"The ones we're going to see," said Qatik. "They're reclaiming."

"Why?" asked Horkai.

Beside him, Qatik shrugged.

They continued on, the houses even sparser now. They

were well into the foothills. Each road they crossed now was carefully labeled, and some minor repair work had been done as well, the road cleared of the larger debris, the largest cracks in the surface filled with dirt and stones. A mile or two more and the houses were gone altogether, the road running along the side of a hill, sloping away to the other side. There were places now where the road was washed out, completely collapsed, and they had to either climb up the hill and through the dust and back down again or clamber down and around. But even here there were signs of someone at work, little hints of a living presence.

An old rest area, rusty metal rail still in place, the building itself having fallen off its foundations to spill into the parking lot. A sudden unbroken run of telephone poles, most snapped off partway down but a few still relatively intact. And then a few more houses, these almost unpleasantly big, at least if their rubble was any indication. Perhaps condos rather than individual houses, impossible now to say. A triangular sign with a silhouette of an animal—a deer, perhaps—crudely painted on it. The corrugated end of an old drainage ditch pipe, now full of blackish ooze, the mountains close enough now that he could see cracks and fissures in the rock face. *How long have we been walking? How much time has gone by?* He looked up to see the sun already well behind them, well on its way to setting.

The road dead-ended into another road, with two metal signs at the end of it. On one, someone had painted in black tar an arrow pointing left and the words s. SASQUATCH BULL. On the other, an arrow pointing right and reading LL COT-TONWD CNY. The two mules consulted, their faceplates close together, gesturing back and forth, and finally went to the right. There was a parking lot, several destroyed cars still in it, and then nothing: only mountains edging down almost to the road, fragments of dead trees, a broken and gravel-edged road.

About two hundred yards along they came to a bare wire, strung at waist height across the road. The mules, seeing it, slowed and then stopped.

"What do you think it is?" asked Horkai.

"A wire," said Qatik simply.

"No," said Horkai. "What is it for?"

Qatik just shrugged.

They got closer. The wire, they saw, hadn't been there long. It was freshly greased and very thin, a slight amber sheen to it.

"Maybe a trigger," said Qanik. "A trip wire."

"A trigger for what?" asked Horkai. "And who would be stupid enough to trip it?"

"I don't know," said Qanik. "During the day nobody would trip it. But at night . . ."

They followed it off the side of the road, careful not to touch it, found that it had been tied to a metal post that had been pounded into the ground. They followed it back in the other direction. There the end of it fed into the lid of a metal box, its outer surface covered with solar panels.

They circled around the box, crossed to the other side of the wire. There seemed no reason to worry about the wire anymore—they'd crossed it and thus it no longer existed. But the mules stayed where they were, examining the wire from the other side, nearly touching it.

Horkai patted Qanik's head. "Come on," he said. "Let's go."

But Qanik shook his head. "We need to set it off," he said. "We need to know what it does."

"That's a stupid idea," said Horkai.

"This is part of our purpose," said Qatik. "This is what we do."

HIVES, THOUGHT HORKAI, lying on the ground a dozen yards away from the mules, watching them squatting by the wire, searching through the backpacks for something. *Mules. Burdens. Purposes.* None of it really made sense: different sets of ideas, different regimes of knowledge that should compete and contrast with one another but which instead had been used by Rasmus to create a sense of community, a sense of duty. Was it only Rasmus or did it go further than that? Was Rasmus a manipulator or was he just as caught in the trap himself?

And now here he was, paralyzed from the waist down, lying in the middle of a canyon road, waiting for something to happen to kill his mules and leave him isolated and stranded.

They'd closed their backpacks again, threw them behind them, toward Horkai. They were speaking to each other, standing very close, one wildly gesticulating and the other holding still, his arms crossed over his chest. They were far enough away that Horkai couldn't hear what they were saying. Then the one that had been gesticulating stalked off the road. A moment later he was back, carrying a large flat piece of shale, as big as Horkai's chest.

Both mules took a few steps back; then the mule with the rock lifted it over his head and hurled it. It caught the wire and instantly snapped it, the ends whipping away.

Horkai, already braced for an explosion, closed his eyes, but no explosion came. Instead, what came was a voice.

"Welcome!" the voice said. *"Welcome, brothers! If you have made it this far, perhaps this is an indication that conditions are sufficiently ameliorated for the human species to*

now survive. We are glad you can survive! But your own personal survival is only the first step. We have been waiting for you, waiting to receive you to let you know what you can do next to help your species.

"*But first a little bit about us. We are here for you. We are here to protect you. We love you, just as God loves you, and we will fight to allow you to survive. God has chosen us to stand attendant to you and to guide you in once again founding civilization. We have waited long for you and you, too, have . . .*"

The message continued on, but a mule had already rushed toward him, scooped him up off the ground, and placed him on his shoulders. They moved down the road, even faster than usual this time. The sound of the voice was quickly lost behind them.

"What's wrong?" asked Horkai.

"It is a trap," said Qatik, from beside him.

"It didn't sound like a trap," said Horkai. "It sounded like a message."

"Traps never seem like traps," Qatik said.

"They said they want to help us."

"No," said Qanik. "Qatik is right. This is a trap. They are not friendly."

"How do you know?"

"We know," said Qanik.

"Besides, the message was not for us," said Qatik. "The message is not meant to be heard for many, many years. It is a message for those who come after us."

"So is it a message or a trap?" said Horkai. "It can't be both. Who told you it was a trap?"

"It does not matter who told us," said Qatik, and Horkai thought, *Rasmus.*

"But if it's a trap, shouldn't we turn around?"

"We can't turn around," said Qanik. "It's our purpose."

"So we're walking into a trap, knowing it's a trap?"

"Yes," said Qatik. "But we have the advantage."

"What advantage can we possibly have?"

"You. You are better than a trap."

CRAZY, HE THOUGHT. He could still hear the voice ringing in his ears: *Welcome! Welcome!* Either it was a trap or it wasn't; in either case, he couldn't help but feel they were going about things all wrong.

They continued walking. No houses at all now, just the weathered and broken white stumps of dead, dry trees. There wasn't as much dust here—either because of the altitude or because the canyon kept it out. WASATCH NATIONAL FOREST, a weathered sign read. As they came closer, it became clear that the lines that composed the letters had been touched up, filled in so they would be visible again. The remains of another road, Horkai noticed, was running beside them and a little above, a little higher up the slope. It veered off and came back again. The sound, not too distant, of a river. If he could see the water, he wondered, would it be as bloodred as the stream he had seen before? To one side, a dozen yards from the road, two piles of carefully cut timber, tree trunks stripped of their branches and bleached now, beginning to crack and separate and flinder away.

And then suddenly they turned a bend in the road and Qatik and Qanik stopped. Horkai looked to understand why, but saw nothing.

"What is it?" he asked. "What do you see?"

"Beautiful," said Qanik, and Qatik answered, "Yes, it is."

They stayed there stock-still. Horkai couldn't see anything

beyond the same broken road, the same cracked trees. And then Qanik and Qatik were moving again, slower this time, drifting to the side of the road.

And then he saw it: just past the asphalt of the road and the gravel of the shoulder, in the dirt: four small, scraggly plants, perhaps four inches tall. They were twisted and contorted in on themselves, their leaves pale and semitransparent, but they were alive: the only living plants that Horkai had seen since going outside.

As they came closer, it became clear not only that the plants were alive but that they had also been planted. They were arranged in a straight line despite the curve of the road itself, and were evenly spaced, perhaps eight inches apart.

Qatik got down on his knees and took a closer look, touching one very delicately, staring at them a long time. And then he got up and Horkai found Qanik lifting him off his shoulders, holding him down as well so that now he could see the individual veins in the leaves, the fine dusting of something not unlike hair on the stalk itself. They had been recently watered; the ground around them was still moist. *What kind of plants are they?* he found himself wondering. And then realized that mattered much less than the fact that they were alive, that they could live outside. And that since they could live, surely others would soon follow.

And then he was trundled onto Qatik's shoulders while Qanik in turn bent down to have a look. He brought his head very close, almost touched them with his faceplate. He turned to Horkai.

"What is their smell?" he asked.

Horkai shook his head. "I don't think they had a smell," he said. "Not that I noticed."

Qanik looked at him for a long moment then turned back to the plants. He stayed there motionless, on his knees, staring.

Finally Qanik got up and gathered the packs Qatik had dropped. Below Horkai, Qatik was coughing, ineffectually holding his hand against his faceplate as if to cover his mouth. Qanik was smiling. "It makes it worth it," he said to Horkai. "Seeing that. Knowing that it can exist. Now I can die in peace."

15

IT WAS NEAR SUNSET when they finally caught a glimpse of Granite Mountain. Perhaps a hundred yards from the road, they could see where the mountain had been cut back to reveal a long wall of grayish white stone. At the base, just visible, the stone had been shaped off and cut in an arch. The arch itself was blocked by some sort of metal grate. It was Qanik who noticed it first, stopping and pointing.

They broke from the road proper, took a steep climb up an unstable shale slope to reach it. As they climbed, Horkai, riding precariously on Qatik's shoulders, watched the rest of the entrance come into view. He realized it was very tall, perhaps fifteen feet high. He could see down it, too, saw that it was a tunnel going back as far as he could see into the darkness. And there wasn't just the one tunnel either, but several, four in all, next to one another, the others becoming visible as they climbed higher. On the outside, bolted to the inner curve of each arch, were a squarish electric light and a buzzing fan, connected by cables to something he couldn't yet see.

They came out in the middle of a parking lot, which had been recently patched and maintained. When they moved close to the first of the tunnels, the light in the arch flicked on. The two mules, feeling overexposed, rushed to the second entrance, and when the light went on there as well rushed past it and toward the mountain itself, flattening themselves against the expanse of stone between the two middle entrances. They were both breathing heavily from the climb. Horkai saw the lights flick off. *Motion sensors,* he thought. The light and fan cables, he saw now, ran out into the parking lot, where they connected to a square box, which was, in turn, connected to a bank of solar panels that covered and blocked off the front half of the lot.

"What now?" asked Horkai.

"What now?" said Qatik. "For us nothing. Now is you."

"You're not coming with me?"

"They will not admit us," said Qatik.

"Why not?"

But Qatik didn't respond.

"But what makes you think they'll let me in?" asked Horkai.

Qanik smiled behind his faceplate. "They will let you in," he said. "You will see."

"After you get through the gate, that is," said Qatik.

"But how do I get in without you?"

"You will have to crawl," said Qanik. "Where is your gun? The Mambo?"

He felt for it, found nothing. "I don't know," he said. "Left it at the hospital, maybe."

Qatik searched through the backpack, pulled out a small short knife. "Put this in your boot," he said. "Just in case you need it."

Qanik nodded. "Do not let them see it. If they see it, they will kill you. Which entrance do you choose?" he asked.

"I don't know," said Horkai. "How should I know?"

"You will have to choose one," said Qanik. "You can only go through one entrance. Perhaps it does not matter which. Perhaps they all go to the same place."

"How do I get past the gate?" Horkai asked.

"Choose an entrance," said Qanik patiently. "If the gate is unlocked, we will lift it up for you. If locked, we will break it open."

"DO YOU REMEMBER what it looks like?" asked Qatik. He was holding him in his arms now, Qanik already straining at the gate. "You remember what Rasmus told you?"

"Silver cylinder," said Horkai. "Red letters on the side. Subzero environment."

Qatik nodded.

He heard, even through the suit, Qanik grunt, and then the sound of him coughing. It went on for a long time. Finally he stopped, took hold of the bottom of the gate, pulled on it again.

"You'll have to help," he said to Qatik.

Qatik crouched down, put Horkai on the asphalt, and joined Qanik. The two mules grunted and strained until finally, with a groan, the gate slid up a foot and a half before jamming.

"Enough," said Qatik. "In you go."

Horkai started crawling toward it. He had to let his breath out and wriggle to make it under, and finally one of the two mules gave him a shove. He was in.

He turned and looked back, regarded the two large figures in hazard suits standing there just on the other side, staring in at him, faceplates pressed against the grate.

"We will wait for you," said Qanik, and then began to cough again.

"Hurry," said Qatik. "Please."

And only then did Horkai realize that something was wrong with Qanik, that something had, in all likelihood, been wrong with him for some time. Not only was he coughing, but he was coughing up blood. The lower part of his faceplate was streaked with it on the inside. *Will he be alive by the time I return?* he wondered.

"Hurry," urged Qatik again.

He nodded, then turned. Dragging his useless legs behind him, he began to pull himself down the tunnel.

THE TUNNEL WAS WIDE AND HIGH, rounded at the top, and continued back for what seemed to Horkai, pulling himself forward by his hands, a very long way. It ran deep into the mountain. The stone of the floor was cool and had been cut straight and polished. It was dusty, but other than that seemed to have suffered no damage.

The hall continued straight back, curving not at all. Every ten yards or so, the light that was now behind him would click off and a light in front of him would click on. He counted six lights before he saw, just beyond the sixth one, a thick metal door, like a door to a vault.

He pulled himself to it. It had neither handle nor hinges, and he wouldn't have known it was a door at all except for the metal frame it was set in. Still, he thought, staring at it, it could just be a panel. It might not be a door at all.

He knocked on it, but his knuckles hardly made a sound. He looked around for something to strike it with but found nothing.

What now? he wondered.

He sat there for a little while, staring at the door, gathering his breath. Finally he struck the door again, slapping it with his open palm this time. The noise it made was only slightly louder.

The light above him went out and he was plunged into darkness. Briefly he was seized by panic, his heart rising in his throat, but the light came immediately back on when he began to wave his arms.

He cupped his hands around his mouth. "Hello!" he yelled as loud as he could. "Let me in!"

The noise resonated up and down the shaft of the hall, but there was no sign he had been heard.

What now? he wondered again. Should he crawl back down the hall and out again, find the mules, get them to open another gate for him? And if that didn't work, would they go on to the next, and then to the final one? And what if that one didn't open either?

He pulled himself over until he was leaning against the wall.

And what if I've been sent on a wild goose chase? he wondered. *What if Rasmus was wrong about what is actually here? What if someone was here but now they're gone?*

But that wouldn't explain the redone road signs, unless whoever had done them had left recently. Even if they had left recently, it wouldn't explain the plants they had seen— freshly watered, not even a day ago. No, someone was somewhere nearby. And with a little luck, they were here.

He cupped his hands around his mouth again, yelled anew. His voice echoed up and down the hall, but again there was no sign that anyone on the other side of the door had heard.

He stayed there, wondering how long he should wait. He was still wondering, when the light switched off again.

This time, frustrated, he didn't bother to wave his arms, just let it stay dark.

There was a hint of something else other than darkness from the far end of the tunnel, the opening out into the night, where the sky was not completely dark but fading fast. There was something else, too, he realized as his eyes adjusted, a strange tint to the darkness around him, not enough to help him see, but something keeping it from being completely dark. He cast his eyes around, looking for whatever it might be, but saw nothing, no crack under or to the side of the door, nothing on the floor or the walls. But it was still there nonetheless, puzzling him.

And then suddenly it struck him. He looked all the way up, at the ceiling, and saw there, above his head, a small red light.

He clapped his hands once and when the light came on saw, on the wall above him, a small camera. As he watched, it made a slight whirring sound, angling differently, looking for something. Looking, he realized, for him.

He knuckled across the floor and to the other side of the hall, where the camera could see him. It whirred for a little longer as it tracked past him. He stared at it, one hand lifted in greeting. Suddenly it stopped, moved to point directly at him.

"Hello," he said to the camera. "Can you hear me?"

The camera didn't move. He turned to determine if it possessed a microphone or speakers, but saw no evidence of either. Feeling helpless, he raised his hands high above his head as if surrendering, then gestured at the door.

Immediately he heard a thunking sound and the door loosened in its frame. As he watched, it swung open a few inches, then stopped. Because of where he was in the hall, all he could see was the door itself, not what lay behind.

"If you have any weapons," said a voice through the crack, "we ask that you leave them outside."

"I don't have any weapons," Horkai lied, stifling the urge to touch his boot and make sure the knife was still there and, if it was, that it was still hidden.

"If you come in peace," said the voice, "you shall find us to be your friends. If you come to make war, you shall find in us formidable enemies."

It was a statement rather than a question, so at first he didn't bother to respond. But when the person on the other side of the door seemed to be waiting he finally said, "Duly noted."

The door swung open a little wider. A hand, hairless and pale and strangely transparent, appeared around the edge of it, extended and open.

"You may enter," the voice said.

Slowly Horkai began to drag himself across the floor. *And now,* Horkai thought, his heart pounding, *we will see what is inside. If it is a trap, then I am walking into it. If it is not a trap, I will take what I came for and leave.*

Jaw set, he pulled himself along. He rounded the door and for the first time saw the man on the other side.

And that was the moment that everything irrevocably changed.

PART THREE

PART THREE

16

THE MAN ON THE OTHER SIDE of the door could have been his double. His skin was exceptionally pale, almost the color of bleached bone. His head was hairless, even the eyebrows missing, and from what Horkai could see—forearms, hands—the rest of his body appeared to be hairless as well. His features, though not identical to Horkai's, were not dissimilar either, and they were roughly the same height. The man was wearing a long tunic, belted at the waist, a pair of worn leather boots below that. Horkai was too surprised to do anything but stare.

The man smiled. "Ah, brother," he said. "You've come home at last."

He lowered his extended hand in Horkai's direction, but Horkai pushed it away. "Can't stand," he said. "Fell off something a few days ago and must have broken my spine."

"No need to worry, brother," said the man. "Time heals all wounds."

"How long since I saw you?" asked Horkai. "Do I know you?"

"You haven't seen me, brother," said the man. "I was

speaking metaphorically. I do not need to know you to recognize that you are my brother. Look at you and then look
at me, and then tell me if you dare that we are not brothers."

Horkai slowly pulled himself over the threshold of the
door and inside, the man stepping a little to one side to let
him enter. On the other side was a small office, four desks in
all. On the wall were the door controls and a small screen
showing what the camera was seeing just outside the door.
A track pad for moving the camera was beside it. The office
itself was lit by a battery of long-stalked LED bundles making up a lamp in the middle of the floor. It gave the room a
stark and unearthly pale glow. The lamp, Horkai saw, had a
hand crank to charge it. On the far side of the room was the
opening of another hall.

"You look exhausted," said the man.

"I am," said Horkai.

"You're lucky I thought I heard something," said the
man. "If I hadn't and you hadn't moved into the camera's
range when you did, I wouldn't have checked again until
morning."

The man pulled the door closed by a handle on the inside, then used the wall switch to trigger the door lock.

He came back over to stand above Horkai, shaking his
head.

"No, no, no," he said. "It just won't do. But if I'm not mis-
taken." And then, lifting a finger, he turned on his heel. He
plucked at one of the light bundles in the lamp and it came
free, battery and all, the end of the bundle still glowing.
He walked briskly across the office and down the hall on the
other end. This, Horkai glimpsed briefly in the light cast by
this makeshift flashlight, was lined with row upon row of
metal cabinets. He watched the light slowly fade down the
hall until it was gone.

Horkai pulled himself over to a chair and then, with great effort, managed to climb into it without tipping it over. From there, he regarded the room. On each desk was an old computer covered in plastic, the plastic dusty enough that it was clear it had been years since any of the computers had been used. He opened the drawers of the desk he was sitting at, found them empty except for a nub of pencil, its tip broken off, and a key chain with no keys on it. The key chain had a representation of a golden figure blowing a trumpet on it, the words FLIRT TO CONVERT etched below.

Flirt to convert what? he thought. What could it possibly mean? The golden figure above the words made him wonder if he'd stumbled upon a relic from some sort of alchemical cult, a Midas cult interested in converting flesh into gold. But that was crazy, wasn't it? And why *flirt?*

And this place, he wondered, looking around, *what was it before?* Storage of some kind obviously, but for what?

He heard a distant clattering noise and a moment later saw light bobbing up the corridor and toward him. The man was pushing something in front of him that gradually resolved from the darkness to become a wheelchair.

"I thought we had one, and I was right," the man said, resocketing the bundle in the lamp. "It's just been sitting back there in storage, but now it has come in handy. Shall we?"

He helped Horkai slide out of the chair and into the wheelchair, making little encouraging but inane comments the whole while. When he realized Horkai was looking at him strangely, he apologized.

"You'll have to forgive me," he said. "It's been a long time since I've had anyone to talk to."

Horkai nodded.

"Now you'll be able to move around on your own power," the man said. "Or I can push you if you'd rather. Maybe a little bit of both?" The man stopped speaking, narrowed his eyes. "By the way," he said, "how did you manage to get here? Surely you didn't crawl the whole way?"

"Of course not," said Horkai quickly. "I had a wheelchair," he said, "but it broke down."

"Where?"

"Not far from here. Maybe a quarter mile back."

"You're still on miles, are you? We thought the ones left alive might have switched to metric by now. Apparently not. I'll go fetch your other wheelchair in the morning," he said, "see if it can't be fixed. Must have been hard going, considering the condition of the roads. I'm surprised you could make it at all. Did you see my plants, by the way?"

Horkai nodded.

"How are they doing?" the man asked. "But excuse me," he said, "we haven't been introduced. Mahonri, same spelling as the prophet, the one who saw the finger of God. And you are?"

"Josef Horkai," said Horkai.

Mahonri gave him a bemused look. "Strange name," he said. "Who are you named after?"

"I don't know," said Horkai. "I'm not sure I'm named after anyone."

"That's odd," said Mahonri. "Here, all of us are named after someone from the Scriptures. You look like us: why aren't you? Shall I give you a new name?"

"You asked earlier about your plants," said Horkai. "They're fine."

"Splendid," said Mahonri. "I'm glad to hear it. Best effort so far: they're still alive."

"The others have died?"

"Of course," said Mahonri. "These will die as well, it's

inevitable, but they're doing better than the last batch. Of course I cheated a little: I started growing them inside."

"Why do you plant them if you know they're going to die?"

"Because someday they won't die," said Mahonri. "And to measure how safe it is outside. It's getting safer for humans. A little safer all the time," he said. "But I'm forgetting my manners," he added. "You don't want to stay out here in the office all night, do you? Shall we go somewhere more comfortable?"

Without waiting for an answer, he plucked another light bundle from the lamp and started back down the hall. Horkai fumbled getting the wheelchair turned around and maneuvering it through the desks, but after a moment was following him down into the hall.

Only it wasn't a hall exactly, he realized once he was in it. It was a vault: crossing through the door, he could see rows of cabinets stretching to either side of him, dozens of rows, maybe more. The one Mahonri took him down was just big enough for his wheelchair; he kept clipping the handles of the lower cabinets, which were hard to see in the near dark. The row seemed to go on for dozens and dozens of yards. He hurried as quickly as he could, trying to catch up.

But Mahonri had stopped, was waiting for him, weirdly lit by the makeshift flashlight he was carrying.

"Incidentally," he said, "how did you know to come here? Did one of us recruit you?"

"I didn't know," said Horkai, realizing he was out of breath. "I just saw that someone had started painting the street signs again and decided to find out who."

"That was me," said Mahonri proudly.

"And then I saw from the road the arch of one of the

openings. "It seemed as good a place as any to go for shelter. It was just luck that brought me."

"It wasn't luck," said Mahonri. "It was God. Look at you. You are our brother, you belong here. God led you here to help us do His work."

Not knowing what to say, Horkai said nothing, trying keep his face as neutral as possible. This seemed to be enough for Mahonri for the time being; he gave a curt smile and turned on his heel, starting down the row again.

They came to a break in the row, a cross-passage that would allow movement to another row. They crossed the break, continued straight on.

"What is in these?" asked Horkai, more as a way to slow Mahonri down than out of any real curiosity.

"Records," said Mahonri. He stopped, turned around. "What we have here is the history of the human race, a record of births and deaths for hundreds and hundreds of years."

"Why?" asked Horkai.

"What do you mean, why?" Mahonri responded. "Humanity is important. All these things must be preserved so that, when the time comes, humanity shall know what it has been, is, and will be."

"When the time comes for what?"

"When the time comes for humanity to return."

"Return from where?" asked Horkai.

"From extinction," said Mahonri. "We're here with the sacred calling of watching over the records, of preserving them and keeping them safe. And now you are here to join us."

"Just records?" asked Horkai, thinking, *How can anything come back from extinction?*

"Excuse me?"

"What about the gardening you've been doing? Or is that on your own time?"

"No . . .," said Mahonri, dragging the word out long. "That's part of it, too. We're much more than clerks. We're keepers." He gave a guileless smile. "Would you like the tour?" he asked.

Horkai hesitated, then nodded.

Mahonri set off again, continuing straight ahead. Horkai banged the wheelchair along the cabinets, trying to keep up.

They came to another break in the row, and this time Mahonri turned right. Horkai followed him past aisle after aisle, until they hit a wall. Here, they turned left.

"This all was meant for records, too," the man said, his voice deadened by the closeness of the cabinets. "But it became clear we needed the space for other things."

The cabinets abruptly ended, the final one mangled and only half there. Mahonri touched a switch, and an LED bulb came on overhead to reveal an open space a little over two hundred feet square, bound by granite walls on two sides. Filling it were eight man-sized storage tanks arranged like the spokes of a wheel. Six were currently iced and buzzing. Around these were a series of sixteen smaller titanium cylinders, each about three feet in diameter and three feet tall. Only four were iced.

"Power was the hardest thing," said Mahonri. "At first there was an emergency generator we could use, but we rapidly ran out of fuel. So, we converted to solar cells. You saw them in the parking lot, no doubt. They're all over the far side of the mountain as well, thousands of panels. Even with that, we still have to keep most of the lights off, and we can never use all the storage pods at once." He looked around him, gestured to the pods. "Lehi's in the one closest to us, followed clockwise by Zarahemla, Teancum, Helaman, Enos, and Jonas. Originally we thought we'd save the tanks for humans, freeze them and use them to start over with later, but we couldn't manage to get any back here without them dying."

"But aren't you human?" asked Horkai.

"Of course not," Mahonri said. "And you're not either. If you were still human, you'd be dead by now."

"If we're not human, what are we?"

"Lots of theological debate over that one," said Mahonri. "You can look at the commentary if you'd like, the notes that each of us makes when the others are asleep—our thoughts on our callings, our religious musings. The Scriptures aren't clear about it. Helaman believes we've had our actual bodies taken away from us, replaced temporarily by organic machines that are neither hurt nor affected by what destroys an ordinary body. Jonas believes that God works by natural means and that he's allowed us to be infected by a polyextremophilic bacterium, some sort of *Deinococcus,* say, or perhaps by a variety of bacteria, and that this has given us our resistance."

"*Dino*-what?"

"Teancum wonders if we're becoming transfigured beings," said Mahonri, ignoring him. "Translated by the finger of God from mortals to immortals. The fact that our bodies seem exceptionally resilient seems to support this, though the fact that we seem also to continue to age, albeit somewhat slower than humans, does not. Enos has been very compelling with his arguments for why we're not human, but seems to have no thoughts on what we actually are."

"And you, what do you think?"

"Me?" said Mahonri. "I think we're the guardian angels of the human race," he said. "We know our calling and we strive to fulfill it. The specifics don't matter much. That's enough for me." He turned and pointed at the storage pods.

"I occupy one of the two remaining pods when one of the others wakes up. You can use the other."

"Why would I want to use the other?"

"You can't stay awake all the time," said Mahonri. "You wouldn't last long enough if you did. If we're going to be any use at all, we have to stay alive until it's safe for humans outside. We'll add more solar panels somehow and work you into the rotation. Instead of being awake for one month and asleep for six, we'll now be able to be awake for one month and asleep for seven. Thanks to you, we'll be alive for eight lifetimes instead of seven."

"Hold on just a . . ." Horkai started, but Mahonri had already turned away, was approaching one of the nonfrosted titanium cylinders.

"Plants," he said. "Seeds. They've all suffered at least slight exposure, but they're resilient. Some might grow. Indeed, as you've seen, some have." He walked over to one of the non-iced titanium cylinders and opened it, beckoning Horkai forward. Horkai rolled up until he was beside it, used the arms of the wheelchair to lift himself and peer in.

There was a series of square plastic baskets inside, stacked on top of one another. Each was full of clear glass bottles, and each of these in turn was filled with seeds, all kinds, all varieties, each bottle carefully labeled.

"Don't need to freeze these," said Mahonri. "Just keep them dry and protected. Though we have a few frozen as well just in case. You can plant a seed that's three thousand years old, and if it's been kept in the right conditions chances are it'll grow. Every once in a while when I wake up, I plant a few, just three or four, not enough to make a dent, not enough that they'll be missed. Usually they don't do much, but as you saw, the last batch is still alive. If this one is still alive when it's time for me to go into storage, I'll leave a note for the person who comes next."

He closed the cylinder, turned back to Horkai.

"Don't worry," he said, patting Horkai on the shoulder. "I'll go over it in more detail before I go into storage. I'll write down what's important, what you need to know.

"And now . . .," he said, turning away, his voice trailing off. He took a pair of cryogenic gloves from where they hung on a hook on the wall and slipped into them. He removed a pair of tongs from its hook as well. He pressed a button on one of the iced cylinders. The lights flickered briefly, then came on a little stronger. The green light on the side of the cylinder went amber, then red.

"After a few moments an alarm sounds," said Mahonri, "so we'll have to be quick." He had worked his hands deeper into the gloves and used them now to force open the cylinder's lid. "The alarm is meant to attract whichever one of us is awake. If that individual doesn't respond quickly enough, then it starts waking us up, one by one."

He reached into the cylinder with the tongs, carefully slid out a small metal cylinder, held it near to Horkai's face. Horkai could feel the cold radiating off it. No red letters on it. "Metal on the outside to protect it from external contamination, glass core inside. I can't show it to you. The sample itself has been coated with cryoprotectants: glycols and DMSO. Should protect the sample for almost a millennium."

"The sample?"

Mahonri looked at him quizzically. "I'm sorry," he said. "I thought you were following me. I thought we were on the same page."

"And what page is that?" asked Horkai, his voice flat.

"You've seen the plants already," said Mahonri. "The seeds. These are the animals: fertilized embryos, thousands of them, from every kind of animal they could get hold of. This is the ark. What we're living through now," he said, gesturing at the walls, "is a modern-day equivalent of the Flood."

"If I remember my Bible, God promised there'd never be another Flood," said Horkai dryly.

Mahonri quickly backpedaled. "Metaphorically, I mean. And technically there's no water. So we can still call it a flood—metaphorically—and yet still understand that God hasn't broken his promise to us."

The alarm had begun to sound, a piercing noise that made Horkai's eardrums throb. Mahonri quickly reinserted the cylinder, closed the vat, and started the cylinder up again. The alarm stopped.

"There you have it," said Mahonri, hanging the tongs back up and beginning to take off his gloves. "Welcome aboard. That's all, really, that there is to see."

"So you have everything ready for when it's safe for humans again?"

"Yes," said Mahonri.

"All the other cylinders are the same?" asked Horkai.

"Well," he admitted, "not all. There are two that you're never to touch."

"Which are those?"

Mahonri's eyes narrowed. "Why do you want to know?" he asked.

"If I don't know," said Horkai, "how can I know to avoid them?"

He watched Mahonri turn the statement around in his head until finally his eyes relaxed and he smiled. "You have a point," he said. He led Horkai to the side closest to the wall and pointed to two of the frozen storage tanks. From the outside, they looked absolutely identical to the rest. Through the lid of one, Horkai saw only a craquelure of ice, opaque, impossible to see through, impossible to glimpse what was inside.

"What's inside?" he asked.

Mahonri shook his head. "It's not for me to say," he said. "There's much you have to learn first. In time you'll be told."

And Horkai, not knowing exactly how to respond to this and unable to think of a way to insist, finally simply accepted this explanation and nodded.

THEY FOLLOWED THE BACK WALL this time, passing the end of each row of cabinets, until they came to another opening. It led onto what was less a hall than a tunnel, the walls rounded rather than squared off, the stone itself unpolished. The wheelchair had some difficulty, and in the end Mahonri grew tired of waiting for him and started pushing him.

How long they traveled down the tunnel Horkai couldn't say. It couldn't have been long, really, perhaps no more than a hundred feet or so. In the end and very suddenly it opened out, spreading into what at first seemed a cavern until Mahonri raised his light and Horkai saw that this, too, was man-made, could see the grooves where the rock had been chiseled and blasted away.

The floor of most of the chamber was covered with water, and Horkai could hear the sound of dripping. He could not see a river or a stream; the water instead seemed to seep in through the rock walls, which were glistening with it.

"It filters in," said Mahonri, noticing Horkai was staring. He fingered the edge of his garment. "It's quite pure by the time it reaches us," he said.

Near the edge of the water was a little makeshift building, made by balancing sheets of corrugated tin against one another, drilling a few well-placed holes in them and bind-ing them together with wire. A stone bench sat just in front of it, the water lapping at its base.

"Welcome to my humble abode," said Mahonri, and bowed.

The front of the shack was open, no wall there at all. Inside the shelter was a cot, an uneasy swirl of blankets on it. Three folding chairs were stacked against the back wall, and on the floor at the head of the bed was another LED lamp. Beside the folding chairs were a dozen or so boxes, in two stacks that almost reached the ceiling.

"Homey," said Horkai.

"I like it," said Mahonri. He pulled up one of the folding chairs and snapped it open. "Some of the others sleep in the archive itself, but I prefer to be here, by the water. One of us will have to sleep on the floor," he said. "Shall it be me tonight? Then you can take tomorrow night, and after that we'll just alternate until you know the system well enough that I can be stored."

"Okay," said Horkai.

"Are you hungry?" Mahonri asked.

Am I? He hadn't thought about it until now, but yes, he did have to admit that he was not only hungry but starving even. He nodded.

Mahonri opened the top box and reached into it. He came out with two packets. He tore these open and then made his way to the underground lake, filling each of them with water.

"It'll be just a minute," he said when he came back and set the packets on the floor. "Which gives us just enough time to pray. Would you like to do the honors or shall I?"

"Uh, you?" said Horkai, caught off guard.

Mahonri folded his arms and bowed his head. He closed his eyes and then began to pray. *"Heavenly Father,"* Horkai heard, sitting there with his arms on his knees and his head unbowed. *"We thank thee for bringing our brother home to help us with our work . . ."* and by that time Horkai was no longer listening, his mind wandering instead, his thoughts only making their way when he heard Mahonri say, *"In the name of thy beloved son, Amen."*

Mahonri opened his eyes and rubbed his hands. "If you don't like the flavor you get, we'll open you another one," he said. He pointed to the boxes. "We've got plenty."

When he handed the packet over to Horkai, its contents had become a thick, gummy paste. It didn't taste like anything. He ate it anyway, sitting in his wheelchair, spooning it into his mouth with his fingers, occasionally exchanging glances with Mahonri, trying to make sense of him.

AFTER DINNER, MAHONRI UNBUCKLED his boots and began to talk. "I don't get the chance very often," he said. "Not to talk to anyone but myself, anyway. After a while it makes a person a little crazy. It's nice to have someone else here."

"I can understand that," said Horkai.

"What did you do before?" asked Mahonri.

"This and that," said Horkai evasively.

"I sold cars," said Mahonri. "Lived in Murray but had a used lot over in West Valley City. Well, it wasn't my lot exactly, but I worked there."

"Where were you when it happened?"

"At home with my wife and child. We immediately went down to the basement and waited. But it didn't do much good. A few hours later, they were covered with sores. A few days after that, they were dead."

"But not you."

"Not me," he said. "Hardly seems fair, does it, but the Lord had work remaining for me here."

"Watching over the records," said Horkai.

"Yes," said Mahonri. "I'm a keeper. As are you now. We are here to preserve things, to help humanity start over again, once it's safe."

"But how do you know things should start over?" asked Horkai. "Maybe it's time for things to come to an end."

"You have doubts, brother," said Mahonri. "It is very difficult to have no doubts, to have faith instead. Faith is the more courageous path."

"Is it?" said Horkai. "Is it really?"

Mahonri ignored him. "It is all written in the Scriptures," said Mahonri, "if you know where to look. The wicked of the earth will be destroyed by war, death, pestilence, and disease, and only then will Christ return and live among us. And then, for a thousand years, there will be no war and the earth shall be changed so that it is again like unto the garden of Eden. There shall be no disease and there shall be an increase in understanding. Satan will have no power over the people, and the righteous shall reign. Has this happened yet? No? Then the world must needs continue until the Second Coming shall arrive."

"You really believe that?"

"I do," said Mahonri, and gave Horkai a steady look. "I know that something touched me and transfigured me so that I might survive where others died. The same is true for you as well, brother. Why would you be alive now were it not for the hand of God?"

Horkai shrugged. "It could be anything. It doesn't have to mean something."

"For instance," said Mahonri.

"For instance, bad luck," said Horkai. "What's more terrible than living when everyone else around you dies?"

Mahonri fell silent, his face suddenly looking remarkably old. "It is a hard path," he finally admitted. "But we would not have been chosen were we not worthy of it. What were you before?" he asked. "What has become of you to make you think this way?"

"I don't know," said Horkai, suddenly tired of lying. "I can't remember much about my earlier life."

"But surely you must have been pure in heart," said Mahonri. "Were you not, you would have perished."

"Stop talking like that," said Horkai. "Stop talking like you're quoting Scripture. You yourself said that we might have survived due to being infected by bacteria."

Mahonri shook his head. "I did not say this," he said. "Jonas wrote it speculatively in the commentary. I merely reported it. And who is to say that God does not operate through natural means? Even if it is a question of infection, could not God have had a hand in it? Could it not be God who infected us?"

They lapsed into silence. *The problem with faith,* thought Horkai, *is that there's no arguing with it. Same problem,* he admitted to himself, *with lack of faith.*

"Am I sure I can trust you?" asked Mahonri, half musing to himself. "Do you have sufficient faith to join us?"

"Let's talk about it in the morning," said Horkai.

17

HE DROPPED OFF ALMOST IMMEDIATELY, falling into a deep sleep almost as soon as Mahonri lifted him off the wheelchair and put him in the cot. He woke up hours later in an utterly pitch-dark room, with no idea where he was. He was filled with panic that he was unconscious again, frozen, deep in storage, but muddled desperately through that to a memory of Mahonri sitting on the floor beside the cot as his eyes closed, reading the Scriptures to himself, half-aloud. Either he was still in Granite Mountain or he'd managed to escape into a dream again. In either case, he lay there, shivering in a cold sweat, his heart beating very fast, the blood pounding in his ears, until at last, little by little, he began to calm down.

He started trying to picture the room in his head, reached out to one side to touch the tin wall beside the bed, adjusting his image of the room accordingly. Mahonri must be here, he realized, lying somewhere beside his bed. He held his breath and listened, heard at last the muffled sound of the other man's breathing.

What now? he wondered.

It was the first time since he'd begun the journey that

he'd had a chance to relax, slow down, think. He imagined Qatik and Qanik still hiding, huddled against the side of the mountain, waiting for him, slowly dying. Or perhaps quickly dying. Or perhaps already dead. What did he owe them exactly? They weren't like him—were, if Mahonri was to be believed, almost another species. He couldn't remember enough about who he was or what his life had been like before the Kollaps to know what he owed them, or owed Rasmus, or owed anyone, for that matter. Had he been, as Mahonri suggested, "pure in heart"? Was that why he'd been singled out, as it were, touched by the so-called finger of God? Not likely, he thought, remembering how he had almost strangled the technician who had awakened him—almost without meaning to, on impulse. No, the last thing he'd been was pure in heart, he was convinced of that.

But what was he now? Was it better that he couldn't remember what he had been before? *A fixer,* Rasmus had called him, but what did that mean exactly? Someone called upon when nobody else could solve a problem and willing to proceed *by any means necessary.* Definitely not pure in heart.

But how did he know that Rasmus was telling the truth? Maybe he hadn't been a fixer at all but simply an ordinary man living an ordinary life: a bank clerk or a high school teacher. Even Rasmus had couched everything he told him in doubt—*my father told me* and *if I get a few of the details wrong, it's because I have them secondhand*—almost as if he expected from the first not to be believed.

He lay staring into the dark, seeing nothing. Whom should he listen to? Whom should he trust? Rasmus, with his hive? The whole structure seemed clearly a sort of mystification, a way of manipulating others for some purpose that Horkai himself couldn't quite see. Was Rasmus the one doing the manipulating, or was he himself manipulated as well? And if so, by whom or what?

He took a deep breath. Too many questions, too few answers. What he did know was that from the beginning Rasmus had not been honest with him, was clearly holding something back. The little he'd been able to get out of the mules didn't tell him much, just confirmed that something was wrong, that he hadn't been told the truth and that maybe they hadn't been either.

But why was Mahonri to be believed instead? A group of seven transfigured men, if they were still men, living deep in a hole within the side of a mountain, guarding what must be millions of records as well as the contemporary equivalent of the ark. And believing that they were acting out God's will, having manipulated Christianity to fit changing conditions. Mahonri was obviously deranged. How could he be trusted? He'd been brainwashed, was clearly a little addled from so much time spent alone. *Finger of God,* Horkai thought. *Not fucking likely. More like the finger of the Devil. Or, even worse, no finger at all.*

So whom did that leave for him to trust?

Nobody. Not even himself, since he had no idea who he really was.

What now? he wondered, and stared up into the dark. Vague shapes were beginning to move across his vision now, vague flashes of light that stuttered back and forth, the result of the effort of his brain to see something when it was too dark to see anything at all.

What were his choices?

He could go off on his own, but without legs he wouldn't get far. Plus there was the disease to consider, the reason he had been frozen in the first place. If that was in fact real and not one lie among many, then there was something to be said for sticking with the people who claimed they were trying to find a cure.

He could stay here with a group of religious fanatics whose only redeeming quality was that they seemed to be suffering from the same physical condition as he, and live largely in storage, allowing himself to be thawed one month out of every eight and participate in the reinstitution of the human race. Something he wasn't exactly sure was a good idea.

Or, finally, he could do as Rasmus and his community had asked, collect a cylinder with red characters on it, whatever secret or special seed it contained, and bring it back.

The first two were dead ends and would get him nowhere. The last was a wild card: something might come of it or maybe nothing. But it wasn't immediately a dead end. Would he ever get answers? Maybe. Would he ever know the whole truth? Probably not. But he had to try.

Which was why, almost without realizing, Horkai had pulled his dead leg toward him with both hands and was now forcing his hand into his boot, groping for his knife.

18

THE DARKNESS WAS CRACKLING with light now, all of it imagined, his optic nerve helplessly convulsing over and over. He reached to the side and touched the wall, tried to imagine himself hovering near the ceiling and staring down at the room from above. There he was, on his cot, and there, behind him, against the other wall, the boxes of dried food. But where was Mahonri? He'd been asleep himself before Mahonri had even lain down. The man could be anywhere.

He rolled very carefully over onto his side, orienting himself as well as he could toward the sound of the man's breathing. He lifted his head, then propped himself up on an elbow. The cot creaked underneath him and he froze, stayed there half-raised, listening. But the breathing didn't seem to have changed.

He placed the knife on the cot just beside him, against his belly. Very slowly he reached out, waving his fingers through the air. They met no resistance. He extended his hand a little farther, did it again. Still nothing. And again, his hand a little more tentative this time, expecting to touch something. Still nothing. He leaned out and down a little, the cot creaking, and extended his arm farther, and this time, halfway along his arc, he brushed something.

It took him a moment to realize it was fabric, a moment more to decide it was the man's tunic. He drew his hand back just a little, moved it back along its arc, stretching a few inches farther. This time he touched something soft and cloudlike that he thought at first was a blanket, then prodded it enough for it to be clear it was a pillow. He stretched farther, lifting his hand, very careful now, and brushed flesh.

He stopped, hesitated, but the breathing hadn't changed. He moved his hand again, inch by inch, until he brushed flesh again and pulled back slightly, then moved it over again, just a little, just a little, until at last he felt the man's breath against the palm of his hand.

He moved the hand down a little, near where he expected the throat to be. He held his hand like that, the muscles in his shoulder starting to tighten uncomfortably as he tried to fix in his mind exactly how far his hand was stretched, where it was exactly. And then, quickly, he drew the hand back long enough to grab the knife.

He lashed out, felt the blade cut, pass through something. Mahonri made a gagging sound and then screamed, his words lost in a fit of choking. Horkai stabbed into the dark again, connected with something, and Mahonri was flailing, striking at his hands, and the knife clattered away. Something struck the cot and overturned it with a bang, and he was trapped between the cot and the wall while, on the other side Mahonri was screaming in earnest, his body thrashing. Horkai pushed the cot into him and tried to clamber over it, but was struck down. And then suddenly he heard the sound of Mahonri up on his feet, stumbling, knocking into the boxes in the back of the room, no longer screaming now but groaning. He heard the slow sounds of the man's footsteps and then something struck the upturned cot and the next thing he knew, something heavy and squirming was on top of him, crushing him, and he was trying to rein in his panic. *Oh fuck,* he thought and struck out once, then again. He groped around, trying to find the keeper's throat, realized he had his hands wrapped around his thigh. He tried to squirm out from under, tried to squirm around, found a hand holding his head down against the floor, his skull beginning to ache.

Just a few inches from his face, the sound of labored breathing, the slight wind of breath, something warm leaking onto his face and neck. The breathing caught and stopped for an instant and then came again, with a sigh. *"Why?"* said Mahonri's voice, little more than a whisper now, barely anything he could hear. And then, without another word, he collapsed.

IT FELT LIKE IT TOOK FOREVER for him to work free of the body. Groping around in the dark, panting and slightly deranged, it took even longer for him to find the wheelchair where Mahonri had folded it up near the front of the shack. The dark was full of figures now, always just out of reach, and as he worked desperately, he felt them swirling around him, surrounding him, brushing their hands over his skin just as he had done to Mahonri. He gave a shiver of revulsion, shook his head. He was beginning to hear voices as well, very quiet, very distant, but still there, and he had started to wonder if Mahonri was really dead after all. Within that haze of panic, he felt like he was shaping the wheelchair out of nothingness, imagining it in the dark, and he was surprised when he finally had it unfolded. He managed to lift himself up into it and found that it held his weight, that it seemed real and he could begin to imagine he might one day be safe.

Carefully, he wheeled along the walls until he felt first the folded chairs, then the pile of boxes, collapsed and scattered now. The floor lamp was harder to find; it had been knocked over in the struggle and he rolled back and forth for some time before finally touching it with a wheel and groping it up. He felt all over it, looking for a switch, but found nothing. Finally, out of desperation, he tore one of the LED bundles free and watched it light up in his hand.

The inside of the shack was a shambles. In one corner, near the cot, the wall itself had been pushed out and the wire holding it together had started to come undone. Mahonri was lying crumpled in the corner, not breathing. Blood was smeared all over the ground and over the boxes in the back, on the wall beside the cot as well. The man's throat was less slit than gouged, torn open just beneath the chin, windpipe gaping. One of his carotids was nicked, the other more or less intact. Horkai looked down and saw that his whole body was drenched in blood.

SHOULD I FEEL GUILTY? he wondered a few minutes later, forcing the wheelchair along. *Should I have regrets?* But whether he should or shouldn't, he didn't seem to have any. *Does that make me a bad person?* he wondered. *But no,* he reminded himself, *according to Mahonri, I'm not a person. I'm not a human at all.*

He couldn't decide if this thought seemed reassuring or was all the more terrifying.

19

IT WAS IMPOSSIBLE TO SEE into either of the two titanium cylinders; their lids were too frosted over. He sat there between them, putting the gloves on, looking at one and then the other, trying to decide which to open. They looked, for all intents and purposes, identical.

Eeny meeny miny mo, he thought, and then chose one. He reached out and turned the unit off and immediately an alarm began to sound. Very quickly he undid the latches and opened the lid, releasing a blast of freezing air.

It was filled with a series of small metal cylinders, each slightly larger and thicker than his middle finger. With the tongs, he turned one around, looking for writing on it, some kind of mark. It was there, but not red; it was blue. He looked at one on the other side of the tank—blue as well.

How long until it starts waking them up? he wondered, listening as the alarm droned on.

Maybe Rasmus had the color wrong, he thought. Carefully he examined another, then another. All blue.

He closed and latched the lid and turned the unit on again. Immediately the alarm stopped. One of the storage units suddenly began making a creaking noise, but whether because it was thawing or freezing again, he wasn't sure.

He turned to the other unit and flicked it off. The alarm began again. He quickly opened it, and this time saw immediately the red characters on one of the metal cylinders inside. He lifted it carefully out with the tongs and moved it carefully into his gloved hand, then closed the lid of the unit, flicked it back on.

This time the alarm didn't stop. One of the storage units was humming now, definitely thawing. How long would it take? A long time, he hoped.

How do I carry it? he wondered, looking at the cylinder, and then had an idea. He removed one of his gloves with his teeth, held it open in his lap, and then dropped the cylinder in. It lodged in the glove's thumb. Carefully he rolled the end of the glove down to seal it and then tucked it into his shirt. Then, spinning the wheelchair around, he moved toward the exit.

THE OUTER DOOR OPENED despite the alarm. He managed to bump the wheelchair over its lip and out into the hall. Turning around, he nudged the door closed, was pleased when it eased its way back into place, though less pleased when he didn't hear the lock click.

A pale light was leaking far into the tunnel. It was dawn or perhaps slightly later. He rolled down the hall as quickly as he could, until he reached the metal grate. From there, he shouted for the mules until finally they lumbered into view.

"Where did you find a wheelchair?" asked Qatik.

"Long story," said Horkai. "We have to go. I had to kill someone back there."

"Did you cut off his head?" asked Qanik.

"What?" asked Horkai, surprised. "No, of course not."

"Then he is not dead," said Qanik. "You always have to cut off the head."

"Doesn't matter now," said Horkai. "Right now all that matters is that you get the gate up and get me out of here before the others wake up."

Qatik looked Qanik up and down, then turned back to Horkai. "I'm sorry," he said. "We can't do it."

"What do you mean you can't do it?"

"Look at us," said Qatik. "Qanik can barely stand. We have eaten nothing for several days. We do not have the strength to lift it farther. We are dying, Josef. You will have to crawl out. You will have to leave your chair behind."

"Do you have the cylinder?" asked Qanik. His face was barely visible now through his faceplate, which was thick inside with smeared blood. Horkai saw Qatik, too, had been coughing up blood, though not quite so much, not yet.

"I've got it," said Horkai.

"All praise be to his name," said Qanik. "Then our purpose can still be accomplished. Our deaths will not be in vain."

ONCE HORKAI HAD SLIPPED OUT of the chair and had gotten his head through, Qatik dragged him the rest of the way out. But it was Qanik who insisted on carrying him.

"No," said Qatik. "You are too sick. You are too dead."

"I can do it now," said Qanik. "For a mile or two. I will not be here to do it later. You need to save your strength for the rest of the way."

And so they set out, the sun to their backs, walking as quickly as they could back the way they had come, Horkai again balanced on Qanik's shoulders. The going was easier now, the road winding downhill. They moved slowly back down the canyon, seeing signs of ruined civilization gradually reappear and thicken. And now, from this direction, Horkai could see, through the haze, to the north, the devastated center of the metropolis, a huge deep crater, maybe a quarter mile across, maybe even wider. He suddenly recalled what it had looked like before, several dozen large buildings, twenty or thirty stories each, and many smaller ones, including the dome of the tabernacle and the six sharp spires of the Mormon temple. Nothing was left now: the buildings that had been within it and all around it were completely gone, reduced to ash. Around that was a belt of ruins—buildings with a few walls still standing, but mostly a field of rubble. Only gradually, far from the center of the blast, did actual houses begin to appear. And then, as the road descended lower, it all fell out of sight.

"Why did they do it?" asked Horkai.

"Why what?" responded Qatik.

"The Kollaps."

Qatik shrugged. "It just happened," he said. "That's what Rasmus says."

"An accident?"

"That hardly seems a sufficient word for it," said Qatik.

Horkai nodded. *These things happen,* he thought, his mind taking a strange turn, *and then we say we didn't mean it, that it was an accident, that it will never happen again. Never again we say: God will not allow it. We say no to torture, and then we find a reason to torture in the name of democracy. We say no to sixty-six thousand dead in a single bomb blast over a defenseless foreign city, and then we do it again, a hundred thousand this time. We say no to eight million dead in camps, and then we do it again, twelve million dead in gulags. Humans are poison. Perhaps it would be better if they did not exist at all.*

. . .

THE SUN ROSE HIGHER, still hidden behind the haze, and as the day went on, the wind rose and the dust along with it. Half the time Horkai was squinting and coughing, trying to breathe through his shirt, despite the blood stiffening it.

"Any water?" he asked.

Qanik said nothing, just kept plodding forward, his steps deliberate and relentless.

"No food either," Qatik said. "Nothing left at all."

Horkai thought again of the water deep within the mountain, slowly trickling out of the rock. It made his throat itch.

"Will we make it back?" he asked.

Qatik, half-turning, took a long look at Qanik and then looked up at Horkai. "One of us will," he said. "Maybe."

HE WATCHED MAHONRI'S PAINTED SIGNS die out, replaced slowly by signs stripped to bare metal, communicating nothing. Lulled by Qanik's awkward but constant gait, he entered a kind of reverie. He thought again of Mahonri, so trusting, believing he was doing the Lord's work, taking a stranger in and falling asleep beside him without a trace of suspicion. He thought again of the way Mahonri had heaved himself up just before collapsing and whispered, *Why?* He wondered if the mules were right, if Mahonri was, even now, lying on the floor of his shack, his wounds sealing, his throat becoming smooth and opaque as his body re-formed itself and brought him back to life. Or if he was simply dead. He thought of the storage units, the alarm going off, the way one of the units had started to thaw, waking up a new keeper. Would the new keeper come after them immediately, while the trail was still fresh, or would he stay and nurse Mahonri back to health, assuming he wasn't dead? *Always cut off the head,* he remembered hearing one of the mules say again—which had it been? Or perhaps they would come after him as a group, four or five at once, hunting him down for what he had done. *No,* he suddenly realized, his thoughts leaping back to an earlier track, *it wasn't that Mahonri let in a stranger; it was that he let in a brother. I look like him. He trusted me because of that. That was why Rasmus needed me for this: not because the keepers wouldn't recognize me, but because they would think they would. As soon as I saw Mahonri, I should have realized.*

"Qanik?" said Horkai. The mule below him had started to weave a little bit. He slapped the side of his hood lightly and the man stopped, then shook himself and continued on, a bit straighter this time.

"Qatik?" said Horkai loudly. "Maybe you should take me now."

Qatik moved closer, touched Qanik's arm. "I am all right," said Qanik, his voice forced out. "I will still carry him."

The mule kept walking, his step a little slower now, a little heavier, a little jerkier, perhaps. He was bent over more, seemed to be staring at his own feet. Qatik stayed close beside them now, just a little behind, keeping close watch.

They kept walking, and Qanik somehow kept going, both Qatik and Horkai growing more and more anxious. The freeway was visible, the road they were on sloping downhill, and Horkai let himself be lulled again by the motion.

"Qatik," said Horkai.

"What is it?" asked Qatik, not looking away from Qanik.

"Have you ever met someone like me?"

"What?" said Qatik. "Like you?"

"Yes," said Horkai.

"Not me personally," said Qatik. "No."

"But you knew the keepers in Granite Mountain looked like me."

"Yes, of course," said Qatik, surprised. "Why else would Rasmus need you?"

They continued on a little way in silence.

"What do you know about me?" Horkai asked.

"What do I know?" asked Qatik. "That you were stored. That you are part of our community. That you are ill."

"If I'm part of your community, then why don't I look like everyone else?"

For a long moment Qatik didn't answer. Finally he said, "You used to look like us, then you changed."

"How do you know this?" asked Horkai.

"Rasmus told—"

"—that's what I thought," said Horkai. "Where did I come from?"

"From a storage unit," said Qatik, finally turning to face him. "You were stored for a long time."

"And before that?"

"I don't know," said Qatik.

"You don't know much, do you?" said Horkai.

Qatik fell silent. "I am a mule," he finally said. "It's not my purpose to know."

"Aren't you curious?" asked Horkai. "Don't you want to know?"

"Yes," said Qatik. "Tell me."

Then it was Horkai's turn to fall silent.

"You are not going to tell me?" Qatik asked. "Is it a secret?"

"No," said Horkai. "It's not that. It's just that I can't remember."

"You can't remember?"

"No," said Horkai.

"Then why did you ask me if I wanted to know?"

"I thought you might know," said Horkai. "I thought you might be keeping it from me."

"Why are you always trying to confuse me?" asked Qatik, his voice anguished.

"I'm sorry," said Horkai. "I don't mean to hurt you. But I have one more thing I need to ask."

For a long time Qatik remained silent, walking along next to them. Finally he raised his hands and said, "All right."

"What do you think I am?" asked Horkai.

"What do you mean?" asked Qatik. "Can't you ask a question I can understand?"

"I changed, you said. That's what Rasmus told you. What I'm trying to ask, Qatik, is if you think I'm still human."

"Is this question a trap?" asked Qatik.

"No, it's not a trap. Just answer honestly."

Qatik shrugged. "You are part of the community," he said. "Beyond that, what does it matter?"

"Just answer the question," said Horkai, his voice starting to rise. "Am I or am I not human?"

"No," said Qatik, turning his bloodstained faceplate toward him. "Of course you're not."

IT TOOK MORE TALKING, more coaxing, but in the end he got a little out of Qatik, almost in spite of the mule himself. No, Qatik told him, Rasmus had taught them that he was not human, but even had Rasmus not said that, Qatik argued, he would have known. Yes, Horkai was part of the community, but he was there to look after them, to protect them.

"A kind of keeper?" said Horkai. "A guardian angel? Something divine?"

"I don't know," said Qatik, clearly uncomfortable. "We did not call you that. We do not know what you are, only what you are not."

"Which is human."

"If you were human, you would be dead by now," said Qatik. "Several times over. It is good that you are not human."

"But what if it's all a lie?" asked Horkai. "What if I don't belong to the community? What if I belong somewhere else?"

"I don't know," said Qatik. "All I know is that the community needs you. We had something we needed and we could not have gotten it without you. Why would you help us if you were not part of our community?"

Why indeed? wondered Horkai. *What game am I playing exactly? Qatik doesn't know anything. Why am I torturing him?*

SOON QANIK BEGAN TO STUMBLE, careening back and forth for a few seconds until, all at once, his legs gave out and he collapsed. Horkai, thrown from his shoulders, scraped his elbow going down, striking the side of his head hard enough to make his skull throb.

He lay there facedown on the ground, feeling his head ache. He turned over to find Qatik kneeling beside Qanik, knocking on his faceplate.

"Wake up, Qanik," he was saying. "Wake up."

He shook him, then shook him again. He lifted one of Qanik's arms and let it fall.

"He's dead," said Horkai.

"Wake up," Qatik said again. "Wake up, please."

"Qatik," said Horkai. "Stop it. He's dead. It's no use."

And so Qatik stopped. Instead he just kneeled there motionless over Qanik, his arms hanging limply by his side.

"I need to bury him," Qatik finally said.

"We don't have time," said Horkai. "You have your purpose to fulfill. They may already be pursuing us."

Qatik shook his head. "I need to bury him," he said again. "I have an additional purpose now, and that is it."

"No," said Horkai. "This is ridiculous. You don't have a shovel. There's no time."

Qatik remained silent, not moving.

"Qatik?" said Horkai. "Are you listening to me?"

Qatik didn't answer.

Horkai sighed. "Qatik, we need to move on."

"Maybe my purpose means nothing," said Qatik. "Just as you have been trying to tell me all along. Maybe my purpose is over now. Maybe I will leave both of you here and go off to have some peace before I die."

"You're not thinking straight," said Horkai quickly. "You're upset, understandably so. This isn't what Qanik would want you to do, is it?" When Qatik nodded, he continued. "Let's compromise. What about the hospital that you took me to when I was shot, the shelter there? We're close to that, aren't we? It's the place where he spent the most time, apart from the community, no?"

"Yes," said Qatik.

"Leave him there down below, in the shelter."

For a long time, Qatik just stayed squatting and staring down at the other mule, stroking his hood softly. "It is not fair," he finally said.

"It's never fair," said Horkai. "Why should it be?"

"All right," he said. He reached down, got his hands under Qanik's legs and back, and, straining, stood up with him in his arms. "The shelter."

"Wait," said Horkai. "What about me?"

"What about you?"

"You can't leave me here."

"One purpose at a time," said Qatik, and strode away.

20

WILL HE COME BACK? wondered Horkai, and then thought, *Why would he? He could just wander off on his own and die.*

No, Horkai tried to tell himself, *he'll come back.*

But even if he does, will he come back soon enough? Even if he comes back, what are the chances of us making it back to the community, to the hive, before he dies?

More important, *Is it safe to be out on the road alone?*

He looked around. On one side of the road was a series of brick walls that looked like they'd been slowly chewed away. A jagged sidewalk ran along beside them. On the other side, a parking lot empty except for two rusted car bodies that had been stacked on top of each other. A storefront behind it missing all its glass, its façade crumbling away. Nowhere to hide.

A little farther along, probably a hundred feet away, he could see what must have once been a small park, the uprights and chains for a swing set, the swing seats themselves long rotted away. A few large rocks. The splintered bole of a large tree. Better than nothing.

He started toward the park, pulling himself along backwards with his arms, dragging his legs. After about thirty feet or so, his hands were hurting, another thirty and they were scraped and bloody. He wanted to stop, kept telling himself that it was ridiculous, that there was no need to be worried, that the keepers probably weren't coming for him, but he kept going. When he left the asphalt and entered the dirt, it was a little better—softer, anyway—but it wasn't long before his hands started to sting. He could see the path his dead legs were leaving through the dirt, two long lines. He tried to brush them over, but that didn't make it look any more natural. *If they're looking,* he thought, *they will find me. There's no point to this.* But he couldn't stop himself from continuing on.

Up close, the tree's bole proved to be wider around than he'd thought. He pulled himself behind it and was almost entirely concealed from the road. Through a crack partway up and before the main break he could see a cross section of the road. He settled in to wait for Qatik's return.

A HALF HOUR WENT by or maybe more; no way to tell. No sign yet of Qatik. Maybe the hospital was farther away than either of them had realized. Or maybe he wasn't coming back after all.

The wind picked up and did more to cover his tracks than all his scraping and struggling had done. Pressed against the trunk, his eyes and mouth were protected, though his throat was still dry and he still felt from time to time the compulsion to cough. *What time is it?* he wondered, and then remembered, again, that a question like that meant little in a place like this. The sun was high above somewhere, largely lost in the haze, perhaps already beginning its descent. That was all he could tell.

And then he heard it, the sound of a voice. At first he

thought it must be Qatik, having come back and now calling for him, searching for him, and he almost shouted and waved. But no, he suddenly realized, this voice wasn't flat enough, wasn't processed by the speaker of a hazard suit. And then he heard another voice respond to it. Both voices, he realized, were speaking loudly, perhaps even shouting, so as to be heard over the wind.

When the voices came again, he realized they were coming closer. There was a long silence. And then a voice spoke again, closer still, and this time he managed to make out its words.

"Brother!" the voice said. "Even now it is not too late! Brother, we believe you were puzzled or confused or perhaps in the grip of nightmare or had grown sore afraid, and that for this you did what you should not! And so we say unto you, there is no lasting harm done. Our brother has been grievously afflicted but he shall not die. Brother! If you hear us, come to us and be one with us in our work!"

The voice fell silent and for a while he heard nothing, and then another voice spoke in its stead, this one deeper, even more booming than the first.

"But if you do not come forth, we shall shake the dust off our feet and curse you. Brother, if you do not stand with us, you stand against us. And those who stand against us are the enemies of God, and the lot of those who are the enemies of God is most dire."

The voice fell silent. There was a brief argument between the two voices, though in tones too low for Horkai to follow.

And then they passed briefly through the portion of the road he could observe through the tree bole. There were three of them, all pale, all bald and hairless, all like him. One was larger than the others and missing an ear, which must have happened, Horkai reasoned, before, while he was still human: otherwise, it would have grown back. They wore dusty tunics, identical to the one Mahonri had worn, and sandals as well. The tall man was arguing with one of the other two, the third trailing slightly behind.

As quickly as they had come, they were past and gone.

"Brother!" he heard one of them shout again, and imagined from behind his bole that it must be the one missing the ear, that he was cupping his hands around his mouth as he walked, calling out to him.

"Brother!" the second voice shouted. "This is your last chance!"

He held himself as still as he could, motionless behind the stump. He listened as the shouts continued and slowly grew distant. *My last chance,* he thought, and wondered, briefly, if he should raise his hand and holler and reveal himself to them. They were, after all, like him.

But what if it was a trap? What if all they wanted to do was coax him out into the open and kill him? He shivered involuntarily against the stump, feeling trapped.

But it was almost as bad, he realized sitting there, if it wasn't a trap. He recalled Mahonri's strange zeal. He'd heard that in the voices of the others as well, in the words they'd chosen, their biblically inflected language. Could he really stand it, a life spent largely in storage, with his few unstored days spent in service of a religious ideal?

No thanks, he thought. *I'd rather take my chances out here with Qatik.*

Where is Qatik? he wondered, and only then did he realize that the mule would be coming back from the very direction that the keepers had been going, that their paths would surely cross.

. . .

WHAT FOLLOWED FELT LIKE HOURS of panic. He imagined Qatik stumbling into them, trying to flee and the large keeper with the missing ear tackling him and crushing his head with a rock. He imagined Qatik hearing their cries and knowing they were coming and then lying in ambush, leaping out at them and killing them. But having his suit torn apart in the process so that he quickly died anyway. He imagined Qatik's head torn from his shoulders and put on the head of a pike, the pike sunk in the center of the road as a warning to others. He would have to crawl back the remaining thirty or thirty-five miles on his own. How far could he make it? A mile?

He was so busy worrying, so busy imagining all the ways in which Qatik must have died and envisioning his own subsequent death, that he almost missed Qatik himself, only accidentally raised his head high enough to see him standing down the road on the spot where he had originally left Horkai, looking desperately around. Horkai pulled his head up above the stump and waved to him. When didn't see him, he shouted his name.

The sound galvanized Qatik, who threw himself down and crawled off the road. He was quickly gone, invisible.

Using his arms, Horkai pulled himself higher on the stump until his head and shoulders and torso were clearly visible from the road. But still he couldn't see where Qatik had gone.

And then he heard from behind him. "It is just you, burden."

He spun around, in the process losing his balance and falling into the dust. Qatik reached down and dragged him up, pressing him against his chest until he could get a better grip. He lifted him onto his shoulders.

"They came," said Horkai. "I had to hide."

"They did not see you?" asked Qatik.

Horkai shook his head, then realized Qatik, below him, couldn't see it. "No," he said. "They didn't see me. What about you?"

"No," said Qatik. "I heard them shouting. They are from the mountain?"

"They must be," said Horkai. "They came looking for me."

Qatik just grunted. He started down the road.

"We'll have to take a different route back," said Horkai. "We can't go down this road."

"We will go south," said Qatik. "There is a large road south near the hospital. We will take that, then try to find the freeway again."

"How do you know they won't turn around?" asked Horkai. "How do you know that we won't run into them?"

"How can I know?" said Qatik. "But if luck is with us, we will hear them before they see us."

AND INDEED NOT FAR from the hospital Horkai did hear them, the sound of their cries. "I hear them," he whispered, patting Qatik on the top of the hood to get his attention, and Qatik dragged him off his shoulders and immediately fled the road. There was a school, but it was set off a little from the road, behind a parking lot. At first, Qatik seemed to be heading for it, but then instead pushed Horkai under a ruined truck. He rapidly rubbed dirt over his suit to dull it, and then fell down beside him.

"Is it safe here?" asked Horkai. "Do we have enough cover?"

"Either we do or we don't," said Qatik. "It is too late now to worry."

"But we could—," started Horkai.

"No more words," said Qatik. "They are coming."

But it was long minutes before they actually arrived, heralded by their voices. Horkai and Qatik stayed there, flat on their bellies, and waited. "Brother!" He could hear them shouting. "Brother!"

"Why do you hide from us?" intoned a voice as the trio came into range. Horkai could see them now from under the shelter of the truck. "Brother, show yourself and join hands with us. Take your proper place beside us." It was the large man missing an ear.

"Brother," said another voice, one of the smaller men. He was distinguishable from the other small man due to the lumpiness of his head. "If you reveal yourself now, things will not go as badly for you as they will if we have to search for you later."

The other man did not say anything for the time being. This man, at least from this distance, looked enough like Horkai that he could have been his actual, rather than his metaphorical, brother. *Did I have a brother?* Horkai wondered. *Do I have a brother?*

He watched the shining backs of their heads as they moved on. "Brother!" shouted the large man again. "We forgive you for what you have done. We do not hold you responsible for what you did to Mahonri. We understand, we swear to you, that it was all a misunderstanding. The man you injured will live. Were he conscious, I am certain he would proffer you his forgiveness and ask you to return with us, to join us in our holy task."

He watched the triune move farther up the road, still shouting, still trying to flush him out, until finally they became inaudible and disappeared from sight.

"Let's go," said Horkai.

"No," said Qatik. "Wait a moment."

And so they waited a time more, crouched under the

rusted hulk of a truck, in the heat and the dust, listening, keeping their eyes pinned on the road.

When after a few minutes the air was still quiet, Horkai repeated his request.

"Yes," said Qatik. "Time to go," and inched out from under the truck. A moment later he grabbed Horkai by a foot and dragged him roughly out as well.

"We will still take the other road," Qatik said. "Just in case."

"All right," said Horkai. He might have said more except Qatik had already forked him under the arms and spun him around, lifting him high and depositing him on his shoulders. This in itself would have simply been business as usual, except for what Horkai saw.

IT HAD BEEN QUICK, just a glimpse; he wasn't exactly certain that he had seen what he thought he'd seen. Qatik had already started off, keeping to one side of the road rather than the middle, just in case the trio decided to double back. He was moving quickly, Horkai's body jogging up and down, but he still managed to bend just a little and lean just a little, and look carefully at the back of the suit's right arm.

A short tear, perhaps an inch or two long, through the suit's outer layer though not through the inner one as far as he could see. Qatik must have done it crawling under the truck. Not so bad as if there were a tear down to flesh, but still, a torn outer layer couldn't shield him as well, would give him, or at least part of him, more unwanted exposure. It would, no doubt, kill him quicker.

Horkai opened his mouth to say something but then stopped himself. Should he say anything? Qatik would be dead soon in any case. If he knew about the tear, would he give up sooner? Besides, it was just his arm, an extremity rather than his torso or head, and so it probably wouldn't make that much difference, probably wouldn't speed up his death much at all. *Or am I just telling myself that because I don't want to have to break the news to him? Guardian of humanity indeed.*

They jounced along, Horkai turning the problem over in his head, trying to understand if there was something he should do, even something he *must* do. But no matter how he looked at the problem, there was always something to make him question each decision. And so, in the end, it was easier to suspend the question, not to make a decision at all. *I'll do it later,* he told himself, and then mentally added *maybe.*

THE ROAD THEY TOOK SOUTH skirted the hospital where they had killed the rogue, where Qatik had presumably left Qanik's body. On the other side were the remnants of a low stone wall, the backs of condominiums visible above it, relatively intact but with their porches rotted off. The road quickly narrowed. They went past the hospital, and behind its parking lots saw a string of clinics and medical facilities, including a collapsed storefront with a jumble of partially melted prosthetic limbs spilling out of it. What was left of a sign a little farther down read

MOUNTA
PEDIA

Like some sort of strange new reference guide, thought Horkai absurdly.

On the other side, the stone wall disappeared and the backs of condominiums were replaced by the fronts of houses.

They crossed another large road. "Shall we turn here?"

asked Horkai. But Qatik said, "No. Not yet." On the far side, instead of houses, there was a large parking lot and large building with a shattered glass front, shelves inside with small bottles on them or scattered all over the floor. *Perhaps a pharmacy,* thought Horkai. And then more houses, the backs of them this time, on a hill twenty feet or so above the roadway. On the other side of the road were neither buildings nor houses but only a steep slope downward. Horkai could see the road rising before them and realized they must be climbing again. Qatik was going slower now, no longer jogging, and Horkai could hear the sound of his ragged breathing crackling through his speaker.

They crossed another road, this one curving quickly out of sight to both left and right. He asked Qatik again if they should take it, but Qatik again said no, not yet. The downward slope to the left of them became even more severe and was bounded now by a metal barrier. From his place on Qatik's shoulders, he could see past it and out over the whole valley.

They came to another crossroads, the other road this time wide and straight. This time when Horkai asked, Qatik said, "Yes, here is where we shall turn." From there they went two miles or so east down a gentle incline to reach the freeway, and then south again along the freeway, climbing uphill again. They passed a huge penitentiary, then something else with a barbed wire fence around it. The light was very dim, the sun having leaked all the way to the west and threatening now to disappear behind the mountains.

"All downhill from here," Qatik told him.

Horkai took this as an invitation to speak. "Do you think there are more?" he asked.

"More?" responded Qatik. "More what?"

"More like me?" said Horkai. "More like them? The ones from Granite Mountain?"

For a long time Qatik didn't say anything, and so Horkai began to repeat the question. But before he was even half-way through, Qatik said, "Yes."

"How many more?"

"I don't know," said Qatik. "At least a few."

"Do you think some have the same disease that I have?"

"Perhaps. Does it matter?"

They continued together in silence, Horkai watching the sun set in the haze, the clouds lighting up like they were bleeding. He patted his shirt, felt the cylinder still secured in the glove's thumb.

"The ones back there," he said after a time, "the ones in Granite Mountain, they thought they'd been saved for a reason. They thought God had chosen them."

"Chosen them for what?" Qatik asked. "To witness the end of the world?"

"As keepers," said Horkai. "Keepers of the human race."

Qatik didn't respond. They kept going. "Crazy, right?" Horkai said.

"I don't know," said Qatik.

"Do you think we will live through this?"

"I've already told you," said Qatik. "I'm already dead."

"No," said Horkai. "I don't mean you and me but humans in general. Is this the end for us?"

"I don't know," said Qatik. And then added, almost as an afterthought, "You are not human."

"I'm sorry you have to carry me," said Horkai. "I'm sorry I've killed you."

Qatik did not answer. Horkai was tempted to leave it at that, but as they continued along, he found something else nagging him, irritating him, until finally, he couldn't stop himself from asking.

"Why did Qanik die so much sooner than you?" he asked.

"We are all different," said Qatik.

"But you told me you were first," said Horkai. "So you have been around longer. Why wouldn't you die first?"

"Because he carried you more."

"Why would that matter?"

"Lots of questions," said Qatik, and gestured to the roadway before him. "Look around you. There is no one here to answer them."

21

WHEN THE SUN FELL, it grew very dark, though perhaps not quite so dark as it had been a few nights before when he couldn't see anything at all. He could now, from time to time, see the outlines of things. Or at least he managed to convince himself he could. The going was a little quicker now, Qatik letting his legs carry him down the slope out of one valley and into the other.

He did not know for certain when he fell asleep, when he started dreaming. One moment he was observing the vague outline of things and feeling the rolling motion of Qatik's gait, listening to the intensity of the quiet. The next he was asleep. He dreamt he was back in a storage tank, not in storage yet but preparing to be stored. The lid of the unit was closed; he was webbed in. The glass itself was clear, not yet frosted over. On the other side of it was a technician, standing by a bank of machinery upon which he would move a level or adjust a slider, as if mixing a song. He was looking at Horkai, waiting for something. Horkai, not knowing what else to do, finally raised a thumb and the technician nodded and smiled. He reached out and touched a button and the storage process began.

In the dream he knew the feet were always the first to go for him, the toes and then the rest of the feet, though he knew other people who claimed it was the hands that went first, not the feet. Then the numbness spread to his fingers and hands and up his legs and arms, slowly converging on the center of his body. The head and chest were always last, but of course he wouldn't feel those; by the time his chest was being stored, he would have been administered an injection to suspend his heart. The head was always frozen quickly after that, almost immediately, so as to minimize damage to the brain.

Everything was fine, everything went well, nothing went wrong, not with the storage, anyway. But outside, something was happening. The technician was no longer there, had simply vanished. In his place he saw Rasmus and the twins, Olaf and Oleg. And one other person, bald and hairless, his back to him.

I'm watching myself, he thought for an instant, but then a moment later was filled with doubts and had to ask himself, *Is it really me?*

As he watched, willing the man to turn so that he could see his face, he saw Rasmus make a gesture that the twins immediately seemed to pick up on. They each took hold of one of the other man's arms and held them tight to his side. Through the glass Horkai heard the muffled sound of his protest, though he was unable to hear the exact words. The man struggled a little, but the twins kept his arms immobilized.

And then suddenly Rasmus lifted his arm and Horkai saw that he was holding a long, very sharp knife.

He must have made an involuntary noise, because for a fraction of a second the twins glanced toward his tank, the man using it as an opportunity to attempt an escape. And, indeed, the man did manage to break free from one twin and was well on the way to breaking free from the other when Rasmus plunged the knife deep into his chest.

Horkai watched the knife come out and then plunge back down. The man screamed and momentarily slumped out of his vision. Then he was up again, struggling and half turning as the knife came down again, and yet again.

And it was only then, as the man grew looser in the twins' grip and finally seemed to lose consciousness altogether—unless, in fact, he was dead—that his head flopped in the right direction and his body turned enough for Horkai to finally get a look.

But what he saw was not what he expected. Instead of seeing his own bloodied face staring back at him, he saw the face of Mahonri. And as he watched, certain that the man was dead, Mahonri's eyes suddenly blinked open. With blood pumping from his chest, he turned to face Horkai's tank, his face wreathed in an unnerving smile.

HE WOKE UP FEELING like he was falling, and had just enough time to realize he actually was. He struck something hard enough to knock the breath out of him.

He must have been unconscious for a few moments, perhaps longer. When he regained awareness, it was to find himself in the dark, listening to someone groaning. It took him some time to realize that the man groaning was in fact him.

His head throbbed. His face was pressed into something dusty and he could taste blood in his mouth. His shoulder ached. He pushed himself over and stared into the dark, trying to remember where he was. Was he in storage still, something having gone wrong? He couldn't feel the walls of the cylinder around him. Dreaming still?

And then he remembered where he was: near a pool in the heart of a mountain, trapped in a shack with a dead man. If the man was in fact actually dead. His skin began to crawl. Where was his knife? He searched the floor beside him, found nothing. He felt around for the cot that he had been sleeping on before it had turned over, but didn't find it. He felt around for a wall, for any of the three walls of the shack, but didn't find those either, touched instead chunks of rock and rubble. Had they been there when he'd gone to sleep? No, he didn't think so—the floor had been clean: Mahonri had been sleeping on the floor and would have swept it clean first. He was sure of that, or reasonably so. He felt around for his own blankets or the blankets that Mahonri had been using, but did not find those either.

And then finally, groping around, his fingers brushed something. Fabric of some kind, a blanket maybe. He passed over it again, brushing it lightly, and then brought his hand down more fully upon it. The fabric, whatever it was, was thick and stiff, not a blanket. The shape was strange, too, and too regular to be just folds in a crumpled blanket.

He took hold of it more firmly and squeezed. There was something inside the fabric and Horkai realized suddenly that he was squeezing a glove.

Just as he realized this, the hand within the glove moved.

He gave a cry and scrambled away as quickly as he could, trying to orient himself in the darkness.

No matter how hard he tried to make it fit, tried to plaster it to the image, he could not picture Mahonri wearing a glove.

That simple fact was enough to open a crack in his perception, to bring everything into doubt, to make his heart slow down, his panic stop. And with that, everything shifted. As quickly as it had sprung into existence, the world that had been building itself up around him in the darkness—the shack, the lake, the dead body on the floor—simply dissolved and was replaced by himself and Qatik, fallen to the ground in the middle of an old freeway.

"Qatik," he asked, "are you all right?"

He heard a groan again, made for it, knuckling backwards over the ground until he found the man's hand again. From there, he worked his way up the arm and to the hood. He shook the mule's shoulders.

"Qatik," he said again.

"What happened?" asked Qatik, his voice slow and thick.

"We fell," said Horkai. "You must have tripped."

Qatik coughed. "I am sorry," he said. "I am weaker. Not paying enough attention. Not enough sleep. Or food. Blood on the inside of the faceplate makes it hard to see."

"No need to apologize," said Horkai.

When Qatik didn't say anything, he shook him again.

"Just need a moment," said Qatik. "I will be all right soon."

"Shall we wait for morning before moving on?" Horkai asked. "When we can see?"

"Can't," said Qatik. "By morning I am dead."

He lay there for a few minutes more, Horkai leaving him alone. Finally he began to move, one of his arms brushing past Horkai's face. His hands were busy at something and then he grunted, and the movements stopped.

"Suit torn," he said, his voice flat and dead.

"Where?" asked Horkai, picturing in his head again the tear on the back of Qatik's arm.

"Belly," said Qatik. "Something went in when I tripped. I am cut, too. Cannot say how bad it is."

And then he fell silent. Horkai waited, trying to see him in the dark, catching only the vaguest hint of his outline. He thought he might have drifted off again. He reached out and felt around, touched him gently on the belly, found the fabric there sticky with blood.

"It's all right if you can't go on," said Horkai.

"Just give me a minute," said Qatik. "I just need a minute."

HE HAD ALREADY BECOME RECONCILED enough to the idea of Qatik's death when the man, grunting, sat up. He groped about until he found Horkai's shoulder, then used it pull himself to his knees.

"How bad is it?" asked Horkai.

"Not good," said Qatik. "But this is not what will kill me." He groped around until he found Horkai's hand and pressed one of the backpacks into it.

"You will help," he said. "You have an additional purpose now. It is this: There is a fusee in here. Find it and break it open."

Horkai felt around the edge of the bag until he found the pull for the zipper. He tugged it open and stuck his hand in, feeling through the shapes until he found a bundle of long, thin tubes. He extracted one, then pulled it out and sniffed it, smelling the garlicky odor of phosphorus.

He carefully felt his way along it until he found where the casing was scored, then quickly cracked it open. It flared up immediately, its light red and blinding, and he quickly tossed it a little distance away.

"Good," said Qatik. "This part is done."

Horkai could see him now, stark in the glow of the flare. The rip in the front of the suit was perhaps four inches long. Blood had spilled down and no doubt was pooling inside it as well. In one hand Qatik held a sharp-edged piece of metal, perhaps part of a signpost, slick with blood. He balanced on his knees, swaying slightly.

"There is an ampoule of morphine and a hypodermic," said Qatik.

"Yes," said Horkai. "Here they are."

"Prime the needle and load it. Push it through the rip in the suit and inject me."

"How much?"

"All of the ampoule," said Qatik.

"Is that a lot?"

"Yes, a lot. You will have to speak to me to keep me awake."

He affixed the needle to the hypodermic. Breaking off the ampoule's tip, he pushed the needle in, drawing the fluid up into the chamber. Carefully he parted the lips of the tear until he could see Qatik's bloody shirt behind it. Rapidly he sank the needle in and depressed the plunger.

Qatik groaned and swayed but did not fall.

"All right?" said Horkai.

"Now," said Qatik. "In the backpack is a plastic bottle of seam sealant."

Horkai searched through the backpack, found it.

"Seal the wound with it, and then the suit."

Horkai took the cap off and pushed the bottle into the opening, spreading the slit wide with his fingers again, turning Qatik a little now so that the light from the fusee would shine on the wound. It was broad and deep, and bits of metal were still in it, blood and fluid oozing around them.

He tried to pick the bits free but Qatik groaned and pushed at his shoulder.

"Just seal it," he said through gritted teeth.

And so he did, squeezing the tube until a translucent substance squirted out of it and filled the wound. It hissed against the flesh, connecting to it, becoming a sort of dark web. He heard Qatik's breathing grow more labored, the muscles around the wound tightening. He squeezed a little more in, then realized that it had started to bind not only to the flesh but to Qatik's shirt as well. He watched it until he was sure the bleeding had stopped and then pulled both sides of the suit's fabric together and sealed them to each other. He held on too long with his fingers and had to tear them bloody to free them.

"All right," said Horkai. "It's done."

"Good," said Qatik, and then made a heaving noise and retched inside his suit. What came up was mostly blood. It gleamed wetly on the inside of the faceplate, slipping down. He reached out and steadied himself against Horkai's shoulder. "I may last another hour or two," he said, and then retched again.

They stayed there for a few minutes longer, until the fusee began to sputter. Using Horkai as a support, Qatik pulled himself fully to his feet.

"Yes," he said. "I think I can do it." He stumbled over to the remains of the barrier edging the freeway, leaned against it, and squatted down.

"You will have to climb on," he said to Horkai. "If you can manage that, I might be able to stand."

Looping the backpack around one arm, Horkai knuckled over to him. Carefully, he heaved himself up until he was precariously balanced on the barrier and then fell on Qatik's back, wrapping his arms around his neck. His legs dangled, scraping the ground. Qatik grabbed them and pulled Horkai's body closer, until he was riding piggyback. Slowly, Qatik straightened up.

When Horkai started to pull himself higher, Qatik said in

a breathless voice, "Not the shoulders. I cannot manage this. Keep your arms tight around my neck and hold on."

THE GOING WAS SLOW. As they moved away from the sputtering fusee, Qatik stumbling a little, the light faded and then was entirely gone. Horkai could see only the wiry ghost of the fusee still burning in his head.

"Can you see?" he asked Qatik.

"A little," said Qatik. His voice was very thick now, slurred. "Not much."

"Shouldn't we wait until morning?"

"No such thing as morning," said Qatik.

He kept on, moving slowly, feeling his way forward when he had doubts. Horkai could not help but think about what might happen if they fell again. Next time, he was certain, they wouldn't get back up.

Horkai began to talk, at first simply urging Qatik on, telling him he could do it, but slowly moving to other things. He spoke of the little he could remember about the Kollaps, offered the scattered bits of it to Qatik, who did not respond back. He spoke of what he could remember about the world before the Kollaps, began to detail what animals could be found on a farm and what they looked like. Why could he remember such things in such detail, reconstruct so many details of the world as it had been, but couldn't remember his own place in it? When he'd finished with that, he began hoarsely to sing, songs he remembered from when he was a child. "The Farmer in the Dell" he started with since it made a good transition from talk about farm animals, then a song about a garbage truck, followed by a long explanation of what a garbage truck was. He started a lullaby but then thought better of it. And then, tired and distracted himself, he slowly fell silent.

When Qatik weaved or stumbled, Horkai would shake his shoulder or strike him atop the hood, and he would straighten up a little. They kept on going, waiting for night to end.

AND THEN SUDDENLY HE WAS BEGINNING to see again, the darkness leaking away and revealing the things hidden within it. At first it was only the shape of Qatik's hood in front of him, but slowly the world became more and more distinct, extending itself around them. *Still hours until sunrise,* he thought, but now at least it was coming. Now at least they could see the road.

Qatik had sped up just a little, not much. He was going forward, stumbling a bit, still weaving a little, clearly confused, sedated.

"Shall I talk to you?" Horkai asked him, realizing how tired he was himself. His eyes felt like they had been squeezed to bursting.

"I feel," said Qatik, "like I'm walking . . ." And then he trailed off.

"You are walking," said Horkai.

". . . underwater," Qatik finished.

"Oh," said Horkai. "Do you need to rest?"

Qatik didn't bother to answer. They kept on, Qatik letting the slope carry him forward, Horkai from time to time shaking him, speaking to him, urging him on.

"Promise me," said Qatik. "Promise me you will finish it. Promise me you will fulfill my purpose. Promise me you will sing to the others what I and Qanik did for them."

"All right," said Horkai. "I promise."

"There is a signal pistol," Qatik said. "A Molins Number 1. A Very pistol. On a belt inside my suit."

"All right," said Horkai.

"When I die, take it, and the signal flares," said Qatik.

"Pull yourself along, as far as you can go, then fire it. Light a fusee, too, so they'll know where to find you. Maybe they will see and come for you."

THE SUN CAME NERVOUSLY OUT, still estranged in dust and haze. The slope slowly leveled off, grew almost flat. Qatik moved forward only with the greatest effort now. He veered slowly off the edge of the road and onto the frontage road, but got tangled in the remnants of a barbed wire fence. It took all Horkai's wits to get him untangled and keep him on his feet. But just when he thought they'd truly reached the end, Qatik tore free with a groan and they were off again, swaying ponderously down the road.

They passed an old salvage yard—unless it was something else and just looked like a salvage yard now. A tattered billboard, little left of it beyond its metal struts. A concrete wall with a window chopped into it, the opening obscured by a metal grille. Pile after pile of dust-covered corrugated piping, a Quonset hut collapsed and blown flat.

"How far away are we?" Horkai asked.

"Far," said Qatik, forcing the word out. "Miles and miles."

And indeed they walked on for what seemed like miles and miles, the sun rising above them, Horkai trying to stay focused, trying to keep Qatik going, goading him on. But he himself was exhausted, his head lolling, and there were a few moments when his hands, tired from hanging on to Qatik's neck for so long, started to slip and he nearly slid off. He was hungry, starving, almost terminally thirsty. He tried not to think about it, tried to stay focused and in control.

They must still have had miles to go when, abruptly, Qatik came to a halt.

"Qatik?" said Horkai.

Qatik stood there swaying back and forth. He took another step, then another. Horkai breathed a sigh of relief that they were going again. But after a half dozen steps, Qatik stopped again.

"Keep going," Horkai urged. "It's not much farther. Your purpose is almost complete."

He heard Qatik retching again in his suit, swaying and nearly toppling, and then the retching suddenly turned to a low, keening laugh.

"My purpose!" he said in a choked voice. "My purpose!"

He took another step and then fell to one knee. "Get up," Horkai told him, striking him lightly on the hood, "get up," and Qatik struggled, tried to get his leg back under him. And indeed, he was already on his way to standing up again when the other leg went and he tipped slowly over and fell.

Horkai rode him down, letting Qatik's body absorb the fall, disentangling himself once they were down. Qatik was lying on one side, moving his hands, motioning with his fingers, almost as if he were typing, but making no effort to get up.

Horkai rolled him faceup and leaned in over him. He tried to catch a glimpse of his face through the faceplate, but it was too filthy with blood spatter for him to see much of anything inside. It was as if someone had been murdered inside—which, thought Horkai, was the case.

"I'm sorry," said Horkai, and was surprised to realize how sincerely he meant it. Qatik tried to raise his hands but couldn't manage it and let them fall. He tried to speak, but his voice was too soft for Horkai to hear. He moved his ear closer to the speaker and asked him to repeat it.

"*Hood*," mouthed Qatik.

What about it? wondered Horkai, and then suddenly got it. "You want me to remove your hood?" he asked.

When Qatik said nothing, Horkai fished a knife out of

the backpack and began cutting through the seam sealant around the hood's edge. Since Qatik still said nothing, he assumed it was what he wanted.

The seal broke away only awkwardly, and he had to roll the flap back and work the fasteners open. His fingers clumsily loosened the hood.

The inside of the hood reeked of blood and vomit. Qatik's thick face was covered with bruises and sores, the flesh itself beginning to lose consistency. His eyes were half-open, fluttering. He looked fragile, extremely vulnerable. Horkai touched the side of his head and cupped his jaw, and Qatik opened his eyes and gave him a worried and frightened look. A look so painfully intimate, it made Horkai want to look away, but he found that he could not.

He saw Qatik's lips move, but heard nothing. He brought an ear down until it was almost touching Qatik's lips and stayed there, hovering, listening until Qatik whispered again.

"Morphine," he whispered.

Horkai moved his head back and nodded, watched Qatik's eyes slip closed. He rummaged through the backpack until he found a sheathed needle, a syringe, and the remaining three ampoules of morphine.

He filled the chamber with the first ampoule and injected it into Qatik's stomach beside the wound, then stayed there waiting. He was about to throw the hypodermic away when he again met Qatik's eyes. Despite the way the man's gaze was already going glassy, Horkai still sensed a mute appeal in it.

He filled the hypodermic with the second ampoule and injected it in the same spot as the first. He stayed looking at the third ampoule, holding it in one hand, the hypodermic in the other. Finally he made up his mind and broke the glass tip off, inserted the needle and drew the morphine up into the reservoir. He hesitated for just a moment over the stomach wound, bringing the needle down to touch the skin and then moving it up higher, injecting it this time into the artery throbbing weakly in Qatik's neck.

A moment later Qatik was dead.

22

HOURS LATER, PULLING HIMSELF along backwards with his arms, night coming on, his hands numb and bloody, he found himself thinking about that moment, that decision. He had been watching Qatik's face as he depressed the plunger, saw almost instantly his already glazed eyes go loose in the sockets, all the tiny little movements of his face falling still. Not more than a few seconds had passed before he was certain that Qatik was dead.

After only a minute or two, the body had already begun to change, becoming a corpse. The skin of the face had grown noticeably paler and the blood had begun to pool, the now bloodless skin draping strangely on the face so that the nose and even the sockets of the eyes became increasingly prominent. He was surprised to find that the limbs weren't stiff at all, not yet, that the muscles instead were completely relaxed.

He had brushed the eyelids closed, then covered the face with the hood, turning the faceplate around until it served as a support for the back of the head. And then he set about cutting through the seam sealant over the chest and belly.

He opened the Velcro, undid the zipper beneath until he could reach his hand in and feel around the dead man's sodden waist and slowly extract the Very pistol and the cartridge belt it was buckled onto. Six one-inch firing flares, plus the three fusees left in the backpack: not much.

He rolled the belt up and put it, the flares, and the Very pistol into the backpack. He undid the backpack's shoulder straps and used them to bind the backpack to his foot, so he could drag it along.

A meaningless death, thought Horkai hours later, covered with sweat and wincing from pain, his arms throbbing as he slowly inched along the freeway, *after a meaningless life.* A man raised to think of himself as having one purpose in life, his whole life leading to and preparing for it. Raised knowing that when the time came for him to fulfill his so-called purpose, the moment of his death would come hand-in-hand along with it. And his purpose? To carry someone somewhere and then carry him back again. To be little more than a beast of burden, hardly even human—something his leader couldn't resist pointing out by calling him a *mule.*

He reached a tear in the road, a disruption that he couldn't drag himself over and had to concentrate on getting around it.

But, then again, he thought, *supposedly I'm not human myself. And my death, when it catches up with me, in a few minutes, a few hours, will be just as meaningless.*

Here he was, alone, in the middle of nowhere, engaged in a task for people who, assuming he did once know them, he did not remember now. And why? Because he wanted to know something about who he was, gain some knowledge that he suspected they might have. Was he committed to some sort of cause? No. Was he opposed to Rasmus and his community? No, not really. Did he side with them? No. He was lukewarm, neither one thing or the other. He didn't feel like he belonged in Granite Mountain any more than he felt he belonged in Rasmus's hive.

But where, then, did he belong?

They don't think of me as an animal, as a mule, he thought. *For them, either I'm an angel or a devil. Maybe a little of both.*

He stopped and wiped the sweat off his face, was sorry he did so when it made his hands sting. He gently patted his hands dry against his shirt, feeling the glove still tucked within it. He took a moment to look around, back at where he had come from. For a long time he had been able to see Qatik's corpse, growing steadily smaller, slowly reduced to a black dot, but now even that had been lost. He looked all around, saw on all sides of him no living thing, not even a cockroach, nothing but wrack and ruin, the ruined monuments of the dead, destruction, marks of calamity, terror, distress. Nothing but him and the Kollaps.

And perhaps they're not wrong, he thought. *Maybe I am a monster.*

And with that, wincing, he stretched his hands behind him and began dragging himself along again.

JUST ME, HE THOUGHT. *I'm the only one left alive.* And indeed, with the sun setting and the lake glittering with a dull red haze, it felt that way. He had left the freeway, was going slowly up a steep hill, past the wreckage of a university, past an old church. The going was tough, almost impossible, and he felt alternately a strange sense of euphoria and exhaustion so intense that at moments his vision dimmed and threatened to die for good. He kept going, kept on, hauling himself up the slope, watching, when his vision wasn't too dim, the sun slowly sinking behind the mountains, darkness slowly gathering itself around him.

. . .

WHEN HE CAME CONSCIOUS AGAIN, it was completely dark. He wasn't certain where he was, why he was sitting up rather than lying down, why he was outside. And then his body took over, continuing the motions it had been making before he lost awareness of himself, his arms throwing themselves out behind him and taking anchor, then dragging his body along. He felt it happening, like he was watching it from somewhere else rather than controlling the body that was doing it, and then, slowly, he felt consciousness bleed away again until he was unsure where he was or what was happening, and whether his body was moving or not, whether he was outside or instead inside, whether he was living and breathing or frozen, in storage, waiting impatiently to come back to life.

WHEN HE CAME CONSCIOUS AGAIN, it was still dark. Was it the same night or another? Was there any way to tell? This time he was lying down, his face pressed against a chunk of rock.

He tried to sit up, found himself too weak and dizzy to manage it. He put his head back down and lay there, gathering his breath, feeling the world slowly starting to spin underneath him, threatening to throw him off its edge.

He clenched his teeth, felt the world briefly stabilize again. Very slowly, he managed to roll over onto his side. He pulled himself around with his arms until he could reach his leg, then pulled it flopping toward him.

Head spinning again, he felt along the leg for the straps of the backpack. Where were they? They weren't there, he was sure of it. Had he lost it? But then suddenly, yes, there they were, his hands had been moving over them the whole time; how had he not noticed?

It took him a long time to figure out how to free the

straps, even longer to pull the backpack toward him until it was close enough to open it. He passed out with his hand thrust down the backpack's throat, came conscious again wondering how much time had passed. Why wasn't it daylight yet? Unless he had passed through daylight already and it simply was another night. *What is in my hands?* he wondered, and then realized that he was grasping the grip of a gun.

He pulled it out, felt out the hammer, the trigger. The barrel was short and thicker than he expected, the opening big enough that he could slip his finger into it.

And then it came flooding back. *Very pistol,* he thought, *flare gun.* He groped again in the backpack until he found the belt, the lumps of the flares studded along it. He forced one out with his fingers but couldn't keep hold of it; it fell somewhere deep into the pack. He started to search for it and then gave up, forcing another flare out of the belt, keeping hold of it this time.

He tugged on the gun's barrel, feeling all around it until he found the breech lock. He levered it open. He tried to force the flare in, but it wouldn't go, and momentarily he thought Qatik had brought the wrong ammunition. But then he turned it over in his fingers and it slid in perfectly.

He closed the breech. The world was starting to feel like it was shifting again, dissolving underneath him. He tried to raise his arm, but found his elbow remained planted against the ground, unwilling to leave it. The gun felt heavy in his hand. *Just drop it,* part of him was saying. *There's no point anyway.*

He managed to take a deep breath. Elbow still planted, he straightened his wrist until he thought it must be pointing straight up. Or straight enough anyway. Raising his head slightly, he pulled the trigger.

The recoil, small though it was, was enough to tear the pistol from his hand, the flash enough to blind him. The flash ran in a slow pattern across his vision, gradually fading as he blinked, and then he saw it, the red glow of the flare far above him, climbing, climbing, and then falling, suddenly going out.

He let his head fall back. He stared up into the blankness. At least momentarily it was less blank, strange flashes of light and blurs of motion started to cross and burst in his vision. The afterimage of the flare, but more than that, too: his mind trying to see in the near total darkness. *Not real,* he told himself, *not real,* and closed his eyes. But they kept on coming, becoming more textured, more real, congealing into abstracted patterns, and then suggestive forms, and finally into faces. Mahonri was there above him, staring down, smiling. And there was Qanik, his face difficult to see behind his faceplate, but also smiling. And, finally, Qatik, pale and dead, but smiling as well.

He closed his eyes but all three were still there. He groped for the flare gun, but couldn't find it. The backpack was there and he searched through it until he found a fusee and pulled it out. He cracked it open, burning two of his fingers down almost to bone, and tried to throw it. It landed not far from his face, close enough that he could feel the heat off it, could smell his clothing burning, unless it was the burnt flesh of his fingers he was smelling, or the burning faces of the dead.

He lay there half-blinded by the light, somewhere between life and death. *Come find me,* he was thinking. *Come find me.*

And then, for all intents and purposes, he died.

PART FOUR

A SENSATION OF COMING BACK *to life, only not quite that: half life maybe. Still utter darkness, though perhaps a faint hint of light on the horizon. A swirl of memory and imagination, a swath depicting a past, real or imaginary, smeared across the inner walls of his skull.*

The darkness spattered with light now, but still nothing visible, no figure distinct from the ground. A tickling in the throat, aching fingers, hunger, well-simulated feelings and sensations, almost as if he were really experiencing them, almost as if he had a body again.

And then suddenly, vague laughter, slowly fading. Words, their sounds murky but comprehensible and properly sequenced—probably real for once rather than imagined— this:

Hey. Hey. Are you still alive? Are you still alive in there?

A woman's voice, something parting his eyelids, a blurred and twisted face, vaguely female. A dull pain that would have been located somewhere in his head, if he still had a head.

Hey, you fired the flare, right? I mean, who else would it

be? Has to be you. And that wasn't so long ago. We both know you're not really dead. You're not the sort to die.

Something moist against lips, trickling into a mouth and pooling against one cheek, trickling down a throat. A hand on a throat, rubbing it, massaging it, until suddenly it convulsed, swallowed.

There we go. Alive after all, aren't you.

It came again, wet, and this time the throat swallowed a little less involuntarily, and he was aware, too, of it as being more than just a throat. He was aware of it as being his throat.

And then just as quickly as this awareness had begun, it flashed away.

WAS HE DREAMING STILL? *He was somewhere, inside now, a blurry space, round, as if he were in the center of a sphere. A vague shape, a face, a woman's face, or no, not quite a woman, not exactly human. Or maybe it was just that his eyes couldn't focus. Hairless? Maybe, or maybe simply shorn short. Eyes not focused enough to do anything. Distant laughter. Something cool and wet touching his face, obscuring his vision.*

Words again, or sounds anyway gradually becoming words. Female voices. But when in this world had he seen a woman? No, he must be hallucinating. Then again, how could a world exist without women? Maybe the rest of it was the hallucination. Maybe this was the only thing that was real. Was he becoming more conscious? Maybe, maybe not. He tried to sit up, felt something holding him down, hands or straps.

. . . anything? one voice finished. What had it been saying before? No, he couldn't capture it.

Just this, *said the other voice.* It was wrapped in his shirt.

Ah, *said the first voice.* How enterprising of him. Shall

we partake? Diversify the field? *Was it a woman's voice after all? He wasn't exactly sure anymore.*

I don't see why not.

Leave him some. Otherwise he'll be disappointed.

He squinted, tried to see them better, but their features remained in flux, something wrong with his eyes, maybe.

Seems to be waking up. Resilient, isn't he?

We all are, at that stage. *At what stage? he wondered. He groaned, tried to sit up again, felt this time the pressure of hands.*

What shall we do with him? *Which voice was that again?* Harvest him?

He's not ready. He's even less ready than the other one.

And yet here he is.

It can't be forced. When it is, results are . . . unstable. Remember what happened to Sarne.

Who is Sarne? he wondered.

So what do we do? *asked the second voice.*

Do? What else can we do?

We throw him back.

A GLARE OF SOME SORT, *the sensation of heat, the smell of dust. He coughed and felt a hand on him, gripping his shoulder, acknowledging him.*

A voice:

There, there. It's going to be all right.

Strange the things that seep their way down to you while you are unconscious, *part of him thought. Or were such things just imagined, a story he was telling to himself, a dream he was dreaming?*

Where am I? Coming out of storage? Coming out of sleep? Dead?

With great effort he managed to open his eyes, saw little more than a blaze of light, furious, scorching the inside of his skull. And then, through it, suddenly bursting, the rough shape of a face, little more than a white circle with two eyes gouged out of it.

Decided to open your eyes, did you?

Face sliding sideways to momentarily block the light. A round head, bald, pale. A mouth with its corners tensed up in a smile.

Glad to see you're coming around.

He tried to speak, but nothing came out. The face gave him a keen look and then leaned closer, so that all he could see was the top of an ear and the side of a head. It was there for a while, while he tried to speak again, and then it moved away, revealed the whole face again.

And then his vision blurred and faded and he felt himself slip away.

A STRANGE SENSATION, *a feeling of light-headedness, a sense of motion, of movement. He heard someone groan, but it took him a while to realize it was him. He willed his eyes to open and they opened, but only very slowly—one of them, anyway.*

He saw the ground moving below him, but farther away than he would have thought. He saw the curve of a man's back, and far below, appearing and disappearing, two booted feet. He was being carried, he suddenly realized, but the person carrying him wasn't in a hazard suit, was neither Qatik nor Qanik. And then he remembered that no, of course it wasn't Qatik or Qanik: both Qs were dead. But if not them, who would it be? And why would they be outside without a suit?

And then he remembered what'd seen earlier: pale head, lack of hair, just like himself.

Oh no, *he thought,* they've found me.

23

HE DREAMED THAT HE WAS IN a world that had been destroyed, subject to a collapse the reasons for which he had a hard time laying a finger on. In this world, something had happened to him to change him, to make him unlike other men—though not only him: there were others, at least a few, who had been through the same transformation as well. In some ways it was a good thing. He was stronger than before, more resilient, very difficult to kill. But in other ways it was less of a good thing: People were frightened of him, would lie to him, would keep their distance. He didn't belong anywhere. Even among those who, like him, had been changed, he didn't feel like he belonged.

But what does that matter? he told himself in the dream. *Who cares if I belong? Certainly I don't care.*

But even as he said it, he felt something gnawing at him. Maybe he did care. Maybe he belonged with humans. Certainly he still felt like he was human. Or maybe he belonged with the others, the ones who looked like him but who thought of themselves as inhuman, as posthuman, as transhuman. *But I still think of myself as human,* he thought.

Why don't they feel they are? And why do humans feel I'm not?

Then the dream focused. He found himself in a rectangular room topped by a dome, pendentives descending to each of the four corners of the room and coming to ground in four separate piers. Irregular ribs radiated in a spiral pattern from the dome's center to gather around a circular opening at the summit. A church, maybe, or some sort of capitol building. It was made of stone, probably granite, and lit only through the opening in the top of the dome itself, and through a series of narrow windows in the rectangular room below. He could hear something, muffled laughter, but when he turned toward where he thought it was coming from, it seemed to be coming from somewhere else.

He moved toward one of the piers. When he touched it, he discovered that what he'd thought was shadow was, in fact, something else, a glutinous gray substance that clung to his hands and fingers and seemed not to want to come off. What he'd thought at first were irregular ribs were lines of this substance, paths made of it, and as he looked closer, he could see a large tadpole-like creature wriggling along one of the paths. What was it? He removed his gun and aimed it, but before he could fire, the creature slithered up the dome and through the hole at the top and was gone.

The scene blurred away and then refocused again, and he was in a large room, but it felt small since it was filled with large metal cabinets that ran to the ceiling, cutting out narrow rows. He was walking down the row, following someone whose face he couldn't see, but he could tell from the back of his head that, just like himself, this man was bald, pale, no longer human. He was muttering to himself, but Horkai couldn't hear what he was saying. He could sense there was something wrong, but couldn't quite figure out what. Overhead, fluorescent lights flickered on, flickered off. He was walking slowly, but the figure in front of him was walking even slower still, and each time he slowed down, the figure slowed down even more so that, little by little, he was coming closer and closer. His feet rang strangely on the floor, and he wondered what it was about the floor, or about his shoes, or about both, that made this so.

He looked down and saw that where he had thought he had the legs of a human he had the legs of a horse or a donkey or some other beast of burden, and they were shivering, struggling to hold themselves upright. The sound he was hearing was the striking of his hooves against the granite floor.

Panicked, he looked back up and saw that where before there had been a keeper there was now a figure wearing a thick black hazard suit, moving awkwardly in front of him, swaying, crashing into the cabinets first on one side then on the other. And then the figure crashed into a cabinet and broke through it, and Horkai saw through the hole a large barren expanse under a burning sun.

The man in the hazard suit turned and gestured for him to follow, and then turned and kept walking. Horkai started to push through the jagged hole but his foreleg caught and tore on the metal lip and he found himself falling, the man in the hazard suit no longer there, nothing there but dust and misery stretching as far as the eye could see.

Lucky for me, he thought in the dream on the way down, *that I'm safe in storage.*

But then he woke up to discover that, for the most part, it wasn't a dream at all.

24

WHEN HE FINALLY WOKE for good, it was to see a face staring down at him, light pouring in through a window behind it. It was a face very much like his own—no hair, no eyebrows, no stubble of beard or mustache, only a smooth pale head, blurry, but coming into focus as he blinked.

"There we are," said a voice soft and smooth as silk. The face it belonged to smiled. At first he thought the face, slender with delicate features, belonged to a woman. And then he wasn't so sure. And then decided it must belong to a man. "How are we feeling?"

He tried to move, groaned, his head throbbing.

The stranger reached out and put an open hand on his chest. "Don't try to get up yet," he said. "All things in their own time. Can you eat?"

He nodded. The stranger disappeared, came back a moment later with a small open jar.

"We'll start easy," he said, and brought the jar close to Horkai's mouth.

"What is it?" Horkai whispered.

"Baby food, more or less," said the stranger. He lifted up

the jar and looked at it. "I made it myself. Some water, some hardtack, a few preserved things that still looked safe. Soaked it all together, mashed it up," He slipped a finger into the jar, brought it back out covered with sludge. "Open up," he said.

At first he shook his head, but the stranger easily slipped his finger into his mouth, forced it through his teeth, held it there until he sucked the finger clean.

"There," said the stranger, "that isn't so bad, is it?" He dipped his finger into the jar again. This time Horkai opened his mouth.

When he'd finished the jar, he was still hungry, felt even hungrier than before he started eating, his mouth watering. But the stranger shook his head. "Who knows how long you were out there," he said. "You have to take it slow. Rest," he said. "Sleep." And then he closed the curtains and left him alone in a darkened room.

HE DID MANAGE TO SLEEP, he wasn't sure how long. When he awoke, the curtain was open, light coming in again, though whether it was the same day or another he couldn't say. The man was beside him again, shaking him slightly. He had another jar, and a spoon this time, as well as a bottle with a bent straw. He hooked the straw into the corner of Horkai's mouth and squeezed the bottle. Horkai felt his mouth flood with water. He swallowed once, then coughed, spluttering it up, then managed to swallow again.

"Too much?" said the stranger, pulling the bottle away. When Horkai kept coughing, he turned him on his side, patted his back until saliva oozed out of the corner of his mouth and he stopped. *Just like when they woke me up from storage,* thought Horkai. "Sorry about that," the stranger said.

When the coughing finally stopped, the man moved him onto his back, held up Horkai's head with his hand as he began to spoon the mush into his mouth. This went better, the mush going down smoother. When Horkai had finished the jar, the stranger smiled. "I'll go get another," he said.

"Are you a keeper?" asked Horkai. "Are you going to kill me?"

"A keeper? I don't know what you mean," said the man. "Why should I want to kill you?" he added, and then left.

"How long have I been in storage?" Horkai asked him when he came back.

"Storage?" said the stranger, a puzzled expression. "But you haven't been in storage," he said.

"But," said Horkai, "I thought—"

"No," said the stranger. "I found you and took you in. You were outside, all but dead."

Then it began to come together, slowly but surely. "You saw my flare?" he finally asked.

"No," said the stranger. "If there was a flare, I didn't see it."

"Who was with you? Who else was talking?"

"Nobody else. Just me."

"There wasn't a woman?"

The stranger shook his head.

"Where did you take me first? Some sort of dome?"

The stranger shook his head again. "I found you and brought you straight here. I didn't take you anyplace else."

"What about Qatik?" asked Horkai. "And Qanik?"

"I don't know what those are," said the stranger, his expression still friendly, still open. "Where they in your backpack?" And then he raised his finger. "There *were* flares in your backpack," he said, "and an old flare gun. But I don't think it had been fired. Also a head."

"A head?" he said.

The stranger nodded. "Someone you killed?"

Horkai shook his head. "I didn't kill him," he said. "The mules did. He tried to kill me."

"Mules, eh? And yet here you are, alive, and there he is, a head in a backpack."

But then what was real and what was not? Either it all should be real or none of it, right? But it was as if he had lived parts of it and dreamed other parts, and the line between the two wasn't something that would be easy to sort out.

"I fired a flare," said Horkai, raising his head, feeling the strain of it. "I'm sure of it. I needed help and I fired a flare."

"All right," said the stranger with equanimity. "If you say so."

He let his head fall back, closed his eyes. "Qatik and Qanik were humans," he said. "In hazard suits. Those are their names. They called themselves mules."

"Ah," said the stranger. "Then they probably weren't in your backpack after all. Were they supposed to be with you? I didn't see them."

His memory, Horkai realized, was confused. Qanik was miles away, dead. Qatik wasn't as far, but far nonetheless; there was no reason the stranger would have seen them unless he'd been traveling farther up the freeway looking for them.

"Who are you?" he asked.

"Do names really matter?" asked the stranger. He gestured around the room with his open palm. "Are you really likely to get me confused with someone else?"

"I'd still like to know," said Horkai.

The man just smiled.

"My name is Josef," said Horkai. "Last name Horkai. You can call me one or the other or both."

"Or nothing at all," said the stranger.

"Please," said Horkai.

"I don't mean to be rude," said the stranger. "It's just that's where we went wrong."

"Where who went wrong?"

"Us," said the stranger. "Back in the Garden of Eden when Adam named first his wife and then the animals. When we started thinking about names rather than the things they were supposed to designate."

"You're a philosopher?" said Horkai.

The man shook his head. "A realist," he said.

"But I have to call you something," said Horkai.

"Ah," said the man, smiling. "A true romantic. All right," he said, "we can compromise." He thought for a moment. "If you want to call me something," he said, "make it Rykte."

"Reek-tah," Horkai repeated. "What kind of name is that?"

"What kind of name is Horkai?" asked the stranger, slightly mocking. "Doesn't that seem at least as improbable?" He dipped the spoon into the food jar, held it out to Horkai, who opened his mouth. "In fact," he said, "*Rykte*'s not a name at all, but a word."

"What does it mean?"

"In this language, nothing. In another, it means 'name.'"

"So your name is *name*?"

"It means not only 'name' but 'rumor.' Also, 'fame, repute, report.' Depending on context, a few other things as well."

"And that's your name?"

"No, it's not my name. It's a compromise," said Rykte. "Now you have something to call me, but I still don't have a name."

HE LAY THAT NIGHT STARING UP at the ceiling, thinking. Where was he? he wondered. Who was this person without a name, this Rykte? What was wrong with him, and where was his community? He didn't feel like he was in danger, but was he? Was he a prisoner?

"Am I a prisoner?" he asked the next day. He was feeling a little better now, could sit up with help and then stay sitting on his own. He could hold the bowl in his lap and bring the spoon down into it and then up again to his mouth.

"What? Of course not," said Rykte. "You can leave anytime you'd like."

"Really?"

"Really," said Rykte. "You can leave now if you want, though I'd suggest waiting until you have recovered a little more."

He took another spoonful of the mush, then another. "I'm sorry," he said. "I didn't mean to accuse you."

"It's all right," said Rykte. "We've all been through a lot."

He nodded, took another spoonful of mush. "Rykte, could someone have taken me before you found me?" he asked.

Rykte stared at him. "I suppose it's possible," he said.

"I remember someone talking," he said. "Two people, talking about me. They took me somewhere and then decided I wouldn't do."

"Wouldn't do what?"

"Just wouldn't do," Horkai said. "I was wrong for whatever they wanted me for."

"And so they took you back outside and left you again," said Rykte.

"It sounds ludicrous when you put it that way."

"What way should I put it?"

Horkai shook his head. "I don't know," he said.

Rykte reached out and touched him on the shoulder. "Is it possible?" he said. "Yes, it is. But I don't know who it would have been or why they would have done it. All I know is that I found you on the freeway and brought you here. You were in a state of confusion, babbling about two women, but also about being in storage. Maybe it all happened, maybe it didn't. Or maybe it happened but just not when you think it did." He smiled. "You're here now. Just hold on to that."

A DAY LATER, HORKAI ASKED AGAIN, "You're not a keeper?"

"You asked me that before. What's a keeper?" asked the stranger. "Do you mean it spiritually, like am I my brother's keeper?"

"No," said Horkai. "A keeper." And then he went on to explain to Rykte about Granite Mountain, the records there.

By the time he finished, Rykte's face was grave. "And this mountain," he said, "is where you came from?"

Horkai shook his head. "No," he said. "I was just passing through."

Rykte shook his head. "We never learn," he said. "What we need is not a cord tying us back to our past, to the long line of disasters building up to this last greatest disaster. What we need is a fresh start."

"They're not people," said Horkai. "They're not human."

"What are they, then?"

"No longer human. They're like us."

Rykte shook his head again, stared at the floor. "You see," he said. "That's the whole problem. Names, categories, divisions. Once you label something, you learn how to hate it. Human, not human. If you're not one, you're the other, and then you and the others can hate each other." He turned to look at Horkai. "You have to understand," he said, "that we're neither human nor not human."

"What are we, then?" asked Horkai.

"We just *are*," said Rykte. "Why can't that ever be enough?"

. . .

OVER THE COURSE of a few days, he got stronger, began feeling better. Soon he was pulling himself from room to room, exploring Rykte's house. It was an old cinder block affair, nothing fancy, five rooms in all. Horkai wondered aloud why he had chosen it rather than something else.

Rykte shrugged. "I grew up here," he said. "When everything collapsed, I didn't see any reason to leave." He looked around. "Had to rebuild most of it," he said, "but it gave me something to do. Finding intact windows that fit was the hardest part of it."

Besides the room Rykte had given to him, there was Rykte's own room, which contained little more than a bed and a dresser, full of simple, practical clothes, a kitchen with cabinets packed with hardtack and preserved foods. A bathroom, with the commode torn out, was now piled with stacks of books. Rykte had built an outhouse back behind the house—though, for the time being, Rykte installed a chemical toilet in the former bathroom for Horkai. There was a sort of living room containing a couch, two armchairs. A credenza to one side of the front door was heaped with guns and knifes, a few grenades as well.

"Just in case," said Rykte, and winked.

In the basement, Rykte told him, he was trying to grow mushrooms, something to supplement their diet. So far without much success. A shed not far from the outhouse served for storage, was filled with anything that Rykte had scavenged that he thought might be useful. He carried Horkai out to it and Horkai was surprised to see only practical things, no relics or mementos to recall past days, just tools, lumber, rope, bits and pieces of metal, rolls of medical tape, vacuum-sealed packets of freeze-dried foods. A hand-cranked distiller surrounded by canister after canister of distilled water.

"What if you run out of food?" asked Horkai.

"There were enough people around here with food storage that at first it wasn't a problem," said Rykte. "Can't see that it'll be a problem in my lifetime. Plus I'm trying to get mushrooms going in several basements around here. Should be okay eventually."

"You're not lonely?" asked Horkai after a few days.

Rykte shrugged. "A little," he admitted. "But I learned early on to keep my distance. Others always want something from you, especially when they realize you can survive outside. Before you know it, they're no longer asking you for something; they're holding a gun to your head and trying to force it out of you."

"Do you feel that way about me?"

"You're welcome to stay as long as you want, if that's what you're asking," Rykte said. "You don't bother me."

"WHAT ABOUT YOUR LEGS?" Rykte asked him a few days later when he saw one of Horkai's legs shivering. "I thought you must have been paralyzed before the change."

"No, not before," said Horkai.

"Well, then they'll come back," said Rykte. "They're already coming back."

"They can't," said Horkai. "I'm ill. If my spine reconnects, it'll travel to my brain and kill me."

Rykte looked at him for a long time, finally shook his head. "Doesn't sound right," he said. "Do you know this for a fact?"

"I was told," said Horkai.

"Is it possible that whoever told you this might have had some reason to lie?"

"It's not impossible," Horkai said.

"I haven't had even as much as a cold since the change,"

said Rykte. "I can drive a rusty nail into my forehead and come away tetanus free. Early on, I lost an eye in a scuffle only to have it grow back a few days later, good as new. We age, but not very quickly, not as quickly as we did before. Whatever happened to our bodies purified them, made them no longer subject to certain conditions that other mortals face. Our bodies have been transformed, and that has made us not only very hard to kill but also very hard to injure."

"And so I'm being lied to?"

Rykte shrugged. "Let your spine grow back together and find out. It's worth the risk."

THE BRIEF QUIVERING IN HIS LEGS was followed by a tingling sensation, then by little jabs of pain. Over the course of a week he tried mentally to will his legs to move, found that they would but not in the way he expected them to, flopping and spasming instead.

Rykte told him not to worry, that everything would come back. He sat beside Horkai, massaging the legs and moving them carefully back and forth, up and down, helping them relearn the movements they had lost.

"What did you do before the Kollaps?" Horkai asked during one of these sessions.

"Why do you say it that way?" asked Rykte, not looking up from his legs. "Why do you pronounce it like it's a foreign word?"

"I don't know," said Horkai. "That's how they say it where I'm from."

"And where is that?"

"I don't know," said Horkai. "I can't remember things very well."

"What did I do?" asked Rykte. "Not much. Went to high school. I was sixteen when things fell apart."

"You watched your parents die?"

Rykte looked up, nodded. "My parents," he said. "My friends, my neighbors, people I knew from school, from church. Those who survived the first blast were afraid of me, and then hated me. A few of them even tried to kill me. And then, fairly quickly, most of them died."

"I'm sorry," said Horkai.

"Why?" said Rykte. "You weren't one of them. You don't have anything to be sorry for."

AFTER A FEW MORE DAYS, his quivering legs learned to hold him upright for a moment or two. Rykte would stand him upright and he would stand there until the legs suddenly gave out and he'd go down, and Rykte would have to catch him. A day after that, he watched Rykte walk away from the house in the early morning, a rifle slung across his back, and disappear. He was gone for several hours, but when he returned he was carrying two aluminum underarm crutches.

"Was looking for forearm crutches," he said, "but I didn't find any. These will have to do."

By late afternoon and after a few falls, he'd learned how to use the crutches. His sides hurt from where the crutch handles rubbed against him, and the web between his thumb and forefinger was growing sore, had perhaps started to blister. But he could move around on his own power.

He made a few turns around the house, then begged Rykte to take him outside.

"All right," said Rykte. "In any case, there's something I want to show you."

. . .

THEY WENT OUT THE BACK DOOR and past the shed. The crutches were a little more difficult to operate in the dirt, but he managed. Rykte took him to the back fence, then carefully pulled off three of the boards, stacking them to one side. He helped Horkai through the opening.

On the other side was a flat expanse of dirt, then a slow slope down to a drainage ditch through which a feeble stream ran. Unlike the other water he had seen, it wasn't red. Looking up it, he could see the end of a corrugated pipe from which the water was coming. In the other direction it went straight for a while then curved before it was lost behind a fence.

"What did you want me to see?" Horkai asked.

"This," said Rykte, and pointed at the stream.

Water, thought Horkai. *So what?* He looked back up at Rykte. "I don't understand," he said.

"Look closer," said Rykte.

And so he did, trying to see what it was about the water that made it different, made it unusual. Was it a little cleaner, a little purer? Maybe, but not enough to make much of a difference. The color was a little strange, maybe, but . . .

And then he realized and almost fell. "Oh my God," he said. It wasn't the water that was a strange color but what was at the bottom of the streambed. There was a thin layer of moss, very pale but there.

"It's very delicate," said Rykte. "Easily damaged. But resistant to the poisons in the air and soil and water. Things are starting to come back, slowly but surely. In another five years, we might even start to see grass. A decade or two after that, and there'll be flowering plants. Tack on a hundred years, we might even begin to see trees. All this will go on in some way or other. The only thing we humans managed to destroy was ourselves."

"But we're not dead yet," said Horkai.

"With a little luck, we will be soon," said Rykte. "We're a curse, a blight. First we gave everything names and then we invented hatred. And then we made the mistake of domesticating animals—almost as big a mistake as that of discovering fire. It's only one step from there to slavery, and once you think of humans as animals—as mules, say," he said, giving Horkai a look, "we become a disposable commodity, war a commonplace. Add in a dominant religion that preaches the end of the world and holy books that have been used to justify atrocity after atrocity, and you're only a step away from annihilation. It's better not to let society develop at all, to leave each person on their own, alone, shivering, and afraid in the dark."

"What are you, a libertarian?" asked Horkai.

"No," said Rykte.

"An anarchist?"

"Who isn't these days?" asked Rykte. "But no, no more so than anybody else."

Horkai looked at him a long time. "You really think humanity should die out?"

"Objectively, yes," said Rykte. "I've thought about it and thought about it, and rationally it seems the right thing. If we want anything at all to go on, humanity should die out." He turned to Horkai and smiled. "But when I think about it subjectively, it doesn't seem so clear cut."

"No?"

"No. So I do nothing. I neither help humanity along toward its own extinction nor do I prevent that extinction from happening. I don't slaughter everyone I meet, don't use well-placed grenades to open the few remaining shelters to the poisons outside. But neither do I help them. What does that make me? Ineffectual? Uninvolved?"

"Lukewarm," said Horkai.

Rykte smiled. *"So then because thou art lukewarm,"* he said, *"and neither hot nor cold, I will spew thee out of my mouth."*

"I've heard that before," said Horkai.

"Of course you have," said Rykte. "It's from the Bible."

"The Bible," said Horkai. "Burn that as well?" he asked.

"Of course," said Rykte, smiling. "It's the cause of more deaths than any other book, including *Mein Kampf.* Better if it had never been written." The smile faded from his face. He turned to Horkai, his eyes hard and serious. "But I guess it's different for you," he said. "You're not exactly lukewarm, are you."

Horkai didn't say anything. They just stood there staring at each other until Rykte clapped his hand down on his shoulder. "Come on," he said. "There's something else I want to show you."

THEY FOLLOWED THE STREAM to where it came out of the pipe and then crossed over the ground behind, Rykte helping him. He heard the noise long before he could figure out where it was coming from, a slow, low droning. He was sweating now, the soreness in his hands becoming blisters, but his legs were already a little stronger, a little more stable.

They traveled up the alley and to the fence in back of another house. Rykte approached the middle of the fence and felt along the boards until one came off in his hands. The ones just to one side of it came off just as easily. He stepped through, gestured to Horkai to follow him.

The noise grew stronger as they approached the house,

growing very loud once he opened the door. They went in; then Rykte came close, spoke into Horkai's ear.

"Leave your crutches against the wall," he said. "I'll carry you the rest of the way."

He put the crutches against the wall, leaning heavily on Rykte. Bending down and pulling him up into his arms, grunting a little, Rykte carried him through the house, down the stairs to the cellar.

The noise was deafening once they were on the stairs. Horkai reached out and touched the wall, felt the vibration. They kept going down, the cellar coming slowly into view.

It was filled with a series of gas-powered generators, perhaps a dozen in all. They were attached by transparent plastic tubes to a water tank in the corner, but Horkai could tell by the color of the fluid in the tubes that it wasn't full of water. The generators were all circuited up to a central converter, which in turn fed their current into a large black cable, which snaked across the floor to a storage tank.

Rykte moved toward it. For a brief terrifying moment, Horkai had the impression that he was planning to put him in it. Instead, he held him over it, mouthed at him to look down.

Horkai did. Expecting to see a stored body, he was surprised when he discovered that the pod was empty, and was again filled with the suspicion that it might be for him.

But it wasn't empty, he realized as he continued to look. There was no body there, but there was still something. A small cylinder with red writing on its side.

"I COULD HAVE DESTROYED IT," said Rykte a few minutes later, when Horkai was back on his crutches and they were moving back to Rykte's house. "But I didn't. Instead I froze it. That's what I've come to see my role as, at least in your case. I won't make a decision about it, but I've preserved your right to make a choice."

He reached out and touched Horkai lightly on the shoulder. "It's been opened. It's been thawed and refrozen. The contents may be damaged," he said. "It may not do any good to give it to whoever you were going to give it to. But then again, it might do a great deal of good, might even allow them a new, fresh start, another generation. You can let humanity go the way of all flesh to extinction, or you can try to help it to keep limping on. So now, what, if anything, will you do?"

"Is it really that important?" Horkai asked. "Can grain really make the difference?"

"Grain?" said Rykte incredulously. He laughed. "There's not grain in there," he said. "Why did you think it was grain?"

"Rasmus told . . .," he started to say. And then he stopped. *Sort of,* Rasmus had said, something like that, when he'd asked if it was grain, or wheat rather. What was the word Rasmus had used? He thought, tried to bring it back, and failed. "If it's not grain," he asked, "then what is it?"

"Fertilized human eggs," said Rykte. "Frozen embryos, ready to be unfrozen and implanted. Humans can no longer reproduce. They've been trying for years. They've been rendered infertile. When I found you, you were carrying the possibility of dozens of humans with you, their whole next generation."

Seed, thought Horkai. That was the word Rasmus had used. *Seed.* He'd stopped moving, was standing in the backyard motionless.

"I'll ask again," said Rykte, "now that you know what you're facing. You may have the key to their continuation. You can give it to them, or you can destroy it. Or you can just wait, do nothing. So many possibilities. What, if anything, will you do?"

25

WHAT WILL I DO? he wondered later, alone in the room he had
already started thinking about as his room. *We name things,*
he imagined Rykte saying, *and then think this gives us the
right to claim them.* The walk had worn him out. His sides
felt bruised, his hands and arms still tingled, and the sensations coming through his feet and legs were broken, irregular. It came and went in waves, getting slowly stronger all
the time. *What will I do?* he wondered again, and thought
of Rasmus, not lying exactly, but very far from telling him
the whole truth. He thought of the keepers, their singleness
of purpose and the almost blithe insouciance that he had
seen in Mahonri, of the way they seemed able to forgive almost anything if they could get one more person (if *person*
was still the right word) to join their cause.

He thought of Rykte and the way he had stepped out of
things, the kind of solitary life he seemed to lead on the edge
of things, a life of apparent profound disengagement. Was it
a life he could live as well?

And then he thought of the technician, the look of fear in
his eyes when Horkai had almost by reflex started to strangle

him. He thought of the several dozen people surrounding Rasmus, dirty and pale and malnourished, none of them much under forty, a whole generation missing beneath them, if not two. He thought of Qanik, comfortable with himself and his role as a mule, stolid and unshiftable in his beliefs. And of Qatik, much less so, a little more acerbic, beginning to be infected by doubt. And of the promise he had made to Qatik before he died.

He thought again about himself, about his past that had been lost somewhere deep within his frozen brain while he was in storage, or perhaps lost in some other way. What had he been? Had he really been a fixer, or was that just another of Rasmus's near lies? Was he a good person or a bad person? *What did I used to be?* he asked himself, and then realized that, no, that wasn't the right question to ask. The right question was not what did he used to be, but what was he going to be now?

BUT TO THAT QUESTION there was no immediate answer. Days went by. At first he worried constantly about his illness, wondering when he'd soon lose all feeling, all sensation. But soon his legs were working again, completely. He was walking without crutches with no sign that he had ever been ill, that he was likely to die, that anything was wrong with him at all. Rykte tested his reflexes, asked him how he was feeling, helped him if he asked for help, but mostly left him on his own.

Some days Horkai would stay in the house, choosing one of the books piled in the bathroom to read, having a discussion or genial argument with Rykte if he was there. Other days he would wander the neighborhood, breaking into empty and collapsed houses, looking at faded family pictures, at piles of bones huddled in the corner of cellars. Some houses were impossible to enter, were completely collapsed or so close to it that he didn't feel he could risk going in. Others, however, had rooms relatively intact. Here a fence would still be standing, but just a few yards away it would be blown flat to the ground, with nothing to indicate why it had fallen in one spot but was still standing in another. It was as if the Kollaps (unless it was simply *the collapse*) had been random and fickle, unpredictable.

Other times he found his footsteps leading him relentlessly back to the other house, the one containing the storage tank. He would remove the boards from the fence and go through, step down into the noisy basement, and then stare through the lid at the cylinder covered in red writing. He would stay there staring, sometimes with his finger touching the switch. But in the end he would always climb back up the stairs and leave without doing anything. Sometimes when he came out, he'd find Rykte in the backyard, as if he'd been following him. He'd look expectantly at Horkai until Horkai shook his head, and then he'd smile just a little and step back through the fence and disappear.

26

LATER, HE REALIZED IT might have gone on like that for years. He might have slowly grown older exploring the neighborhood, reading, looking for signs that life was beginning again, wandering, and every once in a while—less and less as time went on—crossing the irrigation ditch and the fence to stare into the storage tank. But after four or five months, something happened that made everything change.

He had wandered maybe four, maybe five streets away, tracing the way the moss in the stream changed as you continued down it, thicker and greener here, almost entirely gone there, but slowly starting to thicken and spread.

He was on his knees, his face a few inches from the water when he heard something. At first, he assumed it was Rykte, probably out exploring as well, but then he heard a voice.

". . . somewhere around here," he heard the voice saying.

For a moment he assumed it was Rykte speaking to himself, even though speaking to himself wasn't a habit Rykte seemed to have. But there was something wrong with the voice, something strange about it.

And then he heard another voice. It said, "Give me the map."

He got back up to his feet, carefully peered over the remains of the cinder block wall. There, just on the other side, on the roadway, stood two figures in dark hazard suits, rifles slung over their shoulders. They were holding a map between them, both of them bent over it.

"No, no," said the second, pointing. "You see, we turned here. We should have turned here. We have to go that way," he said, and gestured in the direction of Rykte's house.

"Are you sure?"

"Am I sure?" said the second, turning his faceplate toward his companion. "No. But I'm sure this is the wrong place. If you have a better idea, let's hear it."

The first, grumbling, folded up the map, and they started away.

HE FLED QUICKLY BACK along the stream, back toward the house, pushed through the boards and entered through the back door. "Rykte?" he said. "Rykte?"

"What is it?" said Rykte from the front room.

"They're coming," said Horkai. "They're almost here."

"I know," said Rykte, and indeed, when he crossed into the front room, he found that Rykte was already armed, a pistol holstered under one arm and a sawed-off shotgun in his hands. He was standing at the window, which he'd slid open a crack. "Grab what you'd like," he said without looking around, and gestured toward the weapons table.

HE CLUTCHED A RIFLE NERVOUSLY, standing just a little behind Rykte. They saw the two men in hazard suits well before the pair realized which house it was they were looking for, when they were still standing in the street, gesturing again at their map. And then one of the pair pointed straight at their door.

The pair began coming toward the house, casually unhooking their rifles from their shoulders. Before they were halfway across the dirt yard, Rykte shouted, "That's far enough!"

The two men froze, the sun glinting off their faceplates, making their expressions invisible. Horkai wondered if he and Rykte were invisible as well.

"Sling your rifles back on your shoulders," said Rykte. "Or throw them on the ground. Either is okay with me."

The two faceplates turned toward each other and then each put his rifle back on his shoulders. They raised their hands.

"No need to get hostile," said one of them.

"We come as friends," said the other.

"That'd be a first," said Rykte under his breath. "Who sent you?" he called out.

"Who sent us?" said one.

"That's what we were just planning to tell you," said the other.

And then they were silent for so long that Horkai wondered if they expected some kind of response. Rykte, in any case, didn't give them one.

"We know how serious a person you are," said one of them, putting his gloved hand across his heart to show his sincerity. "We know how you love your privacy, and believe me the last thing we'd ever want is to disturb that privacy in any way whatsoever. And yet . . ."

"And yet," the other continued, "here we are. If we are here, it must be important. If we would risk coming here after all these years only to have you point your gun at our heads, it must be very important indeed."

"You haven't told me who sent you," Rykte said again.

"All in good time," said the figure on the left. "All in good time."

"We have to tell it our own way," said the one on the right.

"Tell it, then," said Rykte.

"It'd help us," said Left, "if we knew who we were talking to. Do you mind giving us your name?"

"No names," said Rykte. "Never any names."

"No call to be hostile," said Right. "We've known you so long and yet we don't know what to call you."

"I like it better that way."

"All right, all right," said Left, waving his hands. "We're all friends here, aren't we, Mr. . . ."

"Who sent you?" asked Rykte again.

"Who sent us?" said Left. "We're the same ones as before. There's only one group you ever see, unless there are others we don't know about."

"If I remember correctly," he said, "last time I told you to go away and never come back."

"Something like that, something like that," admitted Right. "And we really did intend to respect your request—have, in fact, respected it for a number of years. How long has it been, Oleg?" he said, turning to the other. "Five years? Six?"

Oh hell, thought Horkai. But in one way he was relieved, glad to know it wasn't Qatik and Qanik back somehow from the dead.

"More like five, Olaf," said Oleg, then turned to Rykte. "You see," he said. "Nothing wrong with calling someone by his name. Olaf and I do it all the time."

"Five it is, then," said Olaf. "Which you have to admit, is a long time, almost as long as forever. And as I said before, we wouldn't have bothered to come now unless we desperately needed you."

"We need your help," said Oleg.

"What kind of help do you need?" asked Rykte. "Food?"

"Well . . .," said Olaf. "Food is good. Nobody can be indifferent to food. But what we're talking about here is a more serious issue of survival."

"There's a mountain," said Oleg. "Made all of granite. Inside the mountain lives a group of beings like you."

"Like me," said Rykte. "What am I like, according to you?"

"You know," said Olaf. "Hairless. More or less impervious. That sort of thing."

"Nice people, I'm sure," said Oleg. "Just like I'm sure you yourself are at heart. Never met them myself. Only heard about them."

"You're getting off track," said Rykte.

"Anyway," said Olaf. "These people stole something, something that we desperately need back."

"We need you to help us get it back," said Oleg.

"We don't travel well. It's too hot out here for us," said Olaf. "We need someone like you."

"Why are you asking me?"

"We don't have anyone else to ask," said Oleg. "Without you, our people will die. Will you help us?"

"Please?" said Olaf.

"No," said Rykte.

"No?"

"Can you really be saying no? We're not asking much of you. Can't you at least think about it?"

Rykte sighed. "All right," he said. "I'll think about it. Come back in five years, and I'll give you my answer."

Oleg turned to Olaf. "He's not taking us seriously," he said in a stage whisper.

"No, he's not," said Olaf.

They turned back to Rykte. "I'm going to ask you again,"

said Oleg. "And this time I'll say please. Did I forget to say please before?"

"You did," said Olaf, "but I said it for you."

"Please," said Oleg. "We need you. It won't take more than a day or two of your time. Please, help us."

Rykte didn't answer; he stayed at the window, brandishing his shotgun.

They waited in silence. Finally, Oleg said, "I'm beginning to get angry."

"Perfectly understandable," said Olaf. "Who wouldn't in our shoes?"

"I'm beginning to wonder what's stopping me from killing you," said Oleg. "You won't help us, you just sit out here on your own, ignoring everybody around you. That's not very neighborly. What good are you? Why shouldn't I kill you?"

"Try it and find out."

"He's right," said Olaf. "You might get one of us, but you probably wouldn't get both of us. There's two of us, and only one of you."

"Actually," said Horkai, "there's two of him."

"Two of him?" said Oleg. "Who said that?"

"I did," said Horkai.

"Do you have a name?" asked Olaf.

"His name is none of your business," said Rykte.

"I recognize his voice," said Oleg. "Is Horkai in there with you?"

"Horkai?" said Olaf. "What are you doing in there? What happened to the mission? Why didn't you come back?"

"It's us," said Oleg. "Oleg and Olaf. You remember us, don't you? We're your friends."

"How could he forget us?" asked Olaf.

"Well put, Olaf," said Oleg. "Horkai," he said. "If it is in fact you, what happened? Couldn't you get in? Were you unable to find the cylinder?"

"You should have at least returned to debrief," said Olaf.

"Did you panic? Go rogue?" asked Oleg.

"Know what happened?" said Olaf. "Weeks after you left, they came. Four of them, or maybe five, hairless bastards just like you but wearing tunics, scarily serene. One of them had a head that looked like it had been crumpled up, eye still growing back, jaw slowly mending, the skin strange and milky in the way that happens with your kind. Wasn't pretty. I'm guessing you did that to him."

"You know who they wanted?" asked Oleg.

"Rhetorical question," said Olaf. "Obviously, they wanted you."

"But they didn't find you," said Oleg.

"No, they didn't," said Olaf. "But that didn't stop them from turning the place upside down. All in the name of goodness and brotherhood, of course, though they weren't above a little casual torture."

"As you'd know if you could see the burns through our suits," said Oleg. "Do we blame you, Horkai? Yes, yes, we do."

"And yet," said Olaf. "And yet, we forgive you. You must have gotten it. You must have taken it from them—why else would they have come looking for you?" He extended a hand. "You should give it to us," he said.

"And return with us to debrief," said Oleg.

"Like a good little boy," said Olaf.

"You boys are getting worked up," said Rykte calmly. "I think it's time for both of you to move along."

"Move along?" said Olaf. "Christ, we were just starting to get somewhere."

"And Horkai wants to come with us, don't you, Horkai?" said Oleg.

"I don't think so," said Horkai.

"Ah," said Olaf. "So it is you."

"What if it is?" said Horkai.

"Ignore them," said Rykte.

"How's your illness?" asked Oleg.

"Still being sure to take steps to prevent it from moving up your spine?" asked Olaf.

"There is no illness," said Horkai.

"No illness?" said Oleg. "No, there's an illness, it just hasn't manifested itself fully yet. What, you stopped taking preventive measures? You think just because you can survive out here, you're immune to everything?"

"You poor deluded soul," said Olaf. "I feel sorry for you."

"There is no—," Horkai had started to say when Rykte's shotgun went off. Horkai jumped. Puffs of dust rose off what was left of a telephone pole over the heads of the pair in hazard suits. Both of them flinched, began patting the fronts of their suits for holes.

Rykte racked the shotgun, the dead shell spitting out onto the floor. "As for me, you'll have to pretty near sever my head to kill me," said Rykte in a steady voice. "For you, all it takes is one hole in your suit. If you hurry for shelter, you might not die, but you'd be more than a little sick for a very long time. Just keep that in mind."

"Why should—?" Olaf started to say, and Rykte fired again, this time throwing up a geyser of dust from the ground near their feet.

"First shot too high, second shot too low," he said. "Did you read 'The Three Little Pigs' when you were young, back before the end of the world? Where do you suppose the next shot is likely to go?" He racked the shotgun. "I think it's time for you boys to leave."

They just stared for a moment and then slowly turned,

left the yard. At the cracked sidewalk, they stopped and spoke to each other, turning back briefly to look at the house. And then, slowly, they went away.

ONCE THEY WERE GONE, Rykte reloaded the shotgun, put it back on the table beside the door. He sat down in a rocking chair, the pistol out of the holster and balanced across his knees.

"That wasn't so bad," he said. "Last time they came, it was worse."

"What happened?" asked Horkai.

"There were a few more of them," he said. "And a few less of us. Had to kill a few of them and deliver the heads back to their friends."

"And then they just left you alone?"

He smiled wryly. "If you deliver enough heads, they tend to do that. At least for a while."

Horkai sat down on the couch. They stayed there like that for some time, not talking. Then, finally, Horkai spoke.

"They'll be back, you know," said Horkai.

"Of course they'll be back," said Rykte. "We haven't killed any of them yet."

"Should we be preparing for them?" Horkai gestured to the pile of guns on the table.

"We're prepared," he said.

"But—"

"They're going to come and we know they're coming. They're planning to try to kill us. We've got weapons, they've got weapons. That's all we can do," he said. He gave Horkai an appraising look. "Unless you want to attack them instead of waiting for them to attack us."

They sat in silence. "This is my fault," Horkai finally said.

"I don't see it that way," said Rykte.

"I told them I'd do something for them. If I go give them what they want, they'll leave us alone."

"Do you really think so?"

Horkai hesitated, then nodded.

"Then you have a better opinion of them than I do," said Rykte. "These are the people who took away the use of your legs. These are the people who lied to you to get you to do something for them in the first place. Do you really think if you give it to them, they'll suddenly change? There is always one more thing. There always will be. You're foolish to go to them."

"If I don't go, they'll just keep coming back. Over and over and over."

"Don't be foolish. They'll do that anyway."

"Maybe," said Horkai. "But not nearly so soon."

Rykte sighed. "You're wrong about all this. It's a stupid idea. But it's your choice." He tucked his pistol back under his arm. "Maybe I'll come with you," he said.

"No, you have no part in this," said Horkai. "I was the one who agreed, I'm the one who should go."

Rykte hesitated, then nodded. "If you're sure," he said.

"I'm sure," said Horkai, although inside he wasn't.

27

LATER, MUCH LATER, just before the end, he had a few minutes to turn all these decisions over in his head, to try to reach an understanding of where and how many times he had gone wrong, to try to figure it out before it was too late, to try to keep a sense of his faults, his errors firmly in his mind at the critical moment so that this time he wouldn't forget them.

But the problem was that, in retrospect, almost every decision he had made seemed like a mistake.

Which one did he regret most? Was it when he first decided to accept the so-called mission, even though he knew something was wrong, that they weren't telling him everything, possibly weren't even telling him the truth? Was it when, inside a mountain made of granite, he had decided to try to kill a man who had been nothing but friendly to him? Or was it when—even though he knew there was no reason for it and every reason against it, even though he knew it was counter not only to his best judgment but to any judgment of any kind, even though he had been warned—he decided to go back and give them what they wanted?

. . .

THE FIRST BIT WAS EASY. Rykte switched off the storage unit, shut down the gas generators one by one. A pair of tongs and a small Styrofoam cooler, and the cylinder was out and ready to travel. Horkai took a pistol and a knife, and then Rykte insisted he take a rifle as well.

"You sure you don't want to reconsider?" asked Rykte as they stood there in front of the house. But Horkai shook his head. Rykte nodded once. "Head for the mountains," he said. "You'll probably see the stadium first, make for that. After that, you should be able to find your way."

They shook hands and then Rykte turned, went back inside.

HE STARTED WALKING toward the mountain, pistol in his pocket, knife in his boot, rifle slung over his back, carefully carrying the cooler in his arms. *Is Rykte right?* he wondered as he walked. *Is it better for humanity to die out?*

He walked until he came to the end of a cul-de-sac, then simply walked past the house at the end of it, kicked a hole in an already-broken fence, and continued on through another former backyard, little more than dust now, to move around another house and come out in another circle, another cul-de-sac. He walked across it and through the remains of a house, using the smear of the sun and the mountains to guide him, to keep him heading east. Two more backyards, a shallow culvert between them, and he was on a larger street, this one running north-south. He hesitated a moment, considering cutting through backyards, but in the end followed the street north half a block and then took it east. Ruined cars, two of them next to each other, nearly scoured of paint but with enough left to tell that one had been red, the other green. *Like Christmas,* he thought absurdly, and was again amazed by what his mind remembered, and what it could not.

It was a residential development, all houses, no apartments. The houses were single-story, brick ranch homes almost identical in appearance, scattered through with a smattering of bungalows and split-level ranches, the latter largely collapsed. The ranch houses, too, were often partly down or missing their roofs. He followed the road up a gentle slope until it curved north to end in a cul-de-sac. He pushed past a house and went east, climbing a steep slope that seemed to give way beneath him almost as fast as he progressed until, panting, he arrived at the top of a crumbling parking lot facing a derelict church.

The front of the church had collapsed, the roof sloping down to touch the ground. He left the cooler on the pavement and climbed this roof, the structure creaking underneath him, until he had a view down to the lake and up toward the mountain. He carefully scanned the foothills until, finally, he saw the stadium, realized he was much farther south than he'd thought. He traced a tentative path through the streets with his eyes, then climbed down and started off again.

THE SUN, HE COULD SEE, was starting its descent, though it was still a few hours from setting. He passed through the remains of backyards, slowly traveling northeast now, stopping, when he had opportunity, to climb a brick wall or a roof and look again and reorient himself.

He came to a river, its water still red, this one with a different sort of plant life running along the bottom of it, long and filamental and recoiling at the touch, almost more animal than plant. One or two water bugs, too, though more like underwater roaches than like the water striders he remembered watching when he was a child. He watched the tendril of a plant suddenly snap itself around one, suck it under. Yes, he thought, life was coming back, but it was coming back as something else, utterly unlike what it had been before. Another few decades, and perhaps it would no longer be a world humans could survive in. Chary of the plants in the water, he walked along the river until he found a place narrow enough to leap across.

From there, he told himself, he would aim roughly for the place on the mountain where the letter had been; that would lead him directly across the university.

It would have been simple. He would have done it, too, except after just a few blocks he caught a glimpse to the south of a large building, the sun glinting off it. It was, he could see even from here, an old town capitol, made of stone, pillars running along the front at regular intervals. Topping it was a metal dome. It reminded him of his dreams.

He stopped and stared for a long time. *What does it matter?* he told himself. *I dreamed about a dome, so what? That doesn't mean it was this dome. I have a purpose, there is no point deviating from it.*

But when he started again, he was moving not toward the university but south, toward the dome.

WELL BEFORE HE ARRIVED, he looped the cooler over one shoulder by the handle, had the rifle out, the safety off. The building, he saw now that he was closer, had partly collapsed, one of the wings little more than a façade. But the middle section and the dome were still intact.

He circled the building once, looking for signs of life. No signs of recent garbage, no plywood or metal sheets blocking the windows, nothing. Most of the windows were broken all or partly out and there were cracks in the walls, some of them big enough to push through. But he decided instead to climb the front steps, go directly in.

The entrance hall was large and long, with a vaulted ceiling made of glass and steel, most of the glass gone now. It opened up into a grand rectangular room with the dome topping it, pendentives stretching down the walls to ground themselves in each corner. There were, just below the dome itself, on the vaulting of each of the pendentives, remnants of old murals, the images themselves little more than ghosts now. Here he could distinguish a human shape, there a bit of what must have been tree or mountain, but if there was a narrative to be read, he couldn't follow it. The arches themselves were studded with stone, rows and rows of stone flowers carved into them. The dome itself was plastered on the inside and he could see remains of a mural there as well, bits of cloud and sky. Windows around the base of the dome gave light.

A circle had been marked on the floor, a thin line of dark stone against the lighter stone, and another circle around it, and one more, this one in a lighter greenish stone cut through with darker lines, the whole of it vaguely giving Horkai the impression of a target. He circled around the circle but did not enter it.

He felt the columns of the pendentives, but they weren't sticky, no gluey gray substance. He looked up at the dome, scrutinized it carefully. Yes, there was something there—dark lines, streaks along the dome, cutting through the remains of the mural. But whether they were natural wear and tear or something else, he couldn't tell. He stayed staring up at the dome, waiting for something to move, but nothing did.

In the end, he passed under one of the arches and moved into the other part of the building. He climbed a mostly intact stairway and circled a stone balcony, having to leap across it in some places, not altogether sure how stable it was. A door marked SENATE CHAMBERS was half off its hinges, its handle stained with blood. He pushed through.

The floor just inside the door was smeared with blood.

Beyond that were collapsed desks and scattered chairs, as well as heaps of black phones. In the front, a dais, a larger desk on it. On it was a body.

He moved carefully forward, rifle ready. The body was relatively recent, not the dessicated corpses he'd seen while traveling with the mules. It was naked. A stake had been hammered into its chest. It was extremely pale and hairless, just like him. He could not tell if it was a man or a woman; the facial features were ambiguous and the hips could have belonged either to a boyish girl or an effeminate man. It had what looked like the beginnings of breasts, but the body itself was chubby and the nipples looked more like those of a man than a woman. Between the legs there was no sex, neither male nor female, but instead what looked like series of a half dozen strings of pearls in a strange gelatinous casing that seemed to have been extruded from the flesh itself. He bent to get a closer look, but couldn't figure their purpose. He was just reaching out to touch them when the creature opened one eye.

He stumbled back, bringing the rifle up, and shot it in the temple. The head jerked to one side and blood began to drip as slow as tar from the hole, and then, even as he watched, the bleeding stopped and the hole turned opaque.

Not dead after all, he thought. He stayed at a distance, wondering what he should do. Part of him—*must be the human part,* he thought—wanted to kill it, wanted to finish the task someone else had started. Another part, though, felt that, whatever it was, it should be given the same chance he himself had been given.

He came close again, this time reached out and tried to tug the stake from the chest. He got it up only a little bit before realizing that the flesh around it had already begun to insinuate it, to make it part of itself. He let it go.

Always remove the head, the human part of him thought. Before it could think anything else, he fled.

HE CUT BACK roughly the way he had come, passing through old yards now reduced to dirt and crossing through ruined fences. He couldn't stop thinking about the creature, wondering what was wrong with it, why it seemed to have sprouted strange appendages in place of its sex. After a while, he had to stop and reorient himself, realized he'd gone too far.

Back to the original purpose, he told himself. *Focus, Horkai.* He came to a surgery center, followed almost immediately by a sprawling medical center, which gave some evidence of being inhabited—nothing he could really put his finger on, just a feeling that things had been arranged, straightened up a little. He thought about exploring it, but in the end gave it a wide berth, thinking of what he'd seen in the town capitol.

He saw a Mormon church, and then, almost immediately, little more than a block away, another one. He saw what must have been a soccer or baseball field—too hard to say now. Another field, all dirt and dust, this one with the cracked remnants of a track encircling it and a set of rotted wooden bleachers. A high school and, fairly close on it, additional fields: the start of the university.

From there it was no time at all before he was standing near the ruined library pounding on the iron door, shouting Rasmus's name.

28

IT WAS SOME TIME BEFORE the door swung open. When it did, it opened to a man in a baggy hazard suit, though of a thinner, less resistant sort than either the mules or the twins had had. When he saw who it was, the man immediately tried to close the door, but Horkai already had his foot in.

"What is it?" asked the man nervously. Horkai could see through the faceplate that the man was thin, old. "What do you want?"

"I need to see Rasmus," said Horkai.

"No," said the man. "I'm sorry. You can't come in."

"I'm here to report," said Horkai. "I've come to report."

"No, I'm sorry, I already told you—"

And that was as far as he got before Horkai butted him in the chest. The man went tumbling backwards, clattering down the steps, and Horkai was in, shutting the door behind him. He went down the steps quickly, stepping over the body of the man, who was groaning and beginning to struggle to get up. He wound down the stairwell to the room below.

They were almost all there, almost the whole community, the whole hive, gathered in the common room at the bottom of the stairs, though they drew back as he came near, as if afraid to be touched by him. He came down to the last step and stood there, holding the cooler in his arms, waiting. It was only after a moment that he became conscious of how many of them were armed, of how many weapons were pointing at him.

"Rasmus?" he shouted. "I've come to report."

The members of the crowd murmured briefly to one another and then fell silent. For a moment nothing happened. He was about to repeat himself when a door in the back of the room opened and out came Rasmus.

He was flanked by Olaf and Oleg, their hoods off but the hazard suits still on.

"You see," said Olaf, when he saw Horkai. "We told you."

"And so you did," said Rasmus. "Hello, Josef. I must admit we weren't expecting you. And walking, too."

"I've come to report," he said again.

"A little late, aren't you? We'd written you off as either dead or a turncoat quite some time ago."

"I have something for you," said Horkai.

"Oh?" said Rasmus. "And what might that be?"

He shook the cooler. "This," he said. He opened the cooler's lid and tilted it so they could see the cylinder inside. "Mission accomplished."

Briefly Rasmus looked dumbfounded, his composure lost for the first time that Horkai could remember. But after a moment he gathered himself again, his face taking on its mask of benign indifference. Then he smiled.

"Well done, Josef," he said. "Why don't you come into my office and we'll talk about how best to reward you."

. . .

IT WAS UNCANNILY LIKE HIS first visit to Rasmus's office so many months before, the only difference being that instead of them easing him into a chair, he was on his feet and could walk to a chair and sit on his own. He instinctively took the chair he'd sat in before, the one behind the desk. Rasmus hesitated a moment, almost said something, then went to sit in the central chair of the three facing the desk, Oleg and Olaf flanking him.

"Comfortable?" Rasmus asked, an edge to his voice.

Horkai nodded. "Good enough for now," he said.

He sat there with the cooler on his lap, Rasmus staring expectantly at him.

"Well?" he said. "You wanted to report. Go ahead and report."

"I have something for you," said Horkai. "I'm going to give it to you and then I'll consider our bargain complete. And then I want you to leave me alone."

"If it's really what we want," said Rasmus, "I imagine we might be able to accommodate you."

Horkai nodded once and put the cooler on the desk. He pushed it toward the trio of men until Rasmus bent forward and took it.

He opened the cooler, looked at the cylinder again.

"It wouldn't survive unfrozen this long," said Rasmus.

"It's been frozen," said Horkai. "I've kept it frozen until now. Though it's probably starting to thaw."

Rasmus reached out and prodded it, quickly yanked his finger away. He closed the lid, handed the cooler to Olaf, whispered in his ear. Olaf nodded sharply, then stood up and left, Oleg following him out.

"They'll handle it," said Rasmus. "We'll get to work immediately, make sure everything is in order. If it is, we can't thank you enough."

"And if it's not?"

Rasmus shrugged. "Then we still have a problem. We'll still need your help."

Horkai shook his head. "I'm done helping," he said.

"Oh?" said Rasmus. "Then why come back at all?"

"To make a good-faith effort to finish what I agreed to do, to tell you that Qanik and Qatik were faithful to their purpose, and to warn you from now on to leave me alone."

Rasmus nodded. "You've been talking to that other one," he said. "The one who won't give his name. What sort of craziness has he been pumping into your head?"

"It's my decision," said Horkai. "It's not him, it's me."

"Josef," he said. "We found you. My father found you. We stored you for years, sometimes diverting power sorely needed for other things to keep you alive. Despite your difference, we made you part of our community—"

"—your hive," he interrupted.

"Yes," said Rasmus, "sometimes we call it a hive. What does that matter? What matters is that we took you in and looked out for you and made you one of us. And now you intend to leave us without repaying us for your kindness?"

"Did that kindness include lying to me about an illness and then crippling me?"

"I told you before, anything I knew about you, I had from my father. I only know what he told me, which was what you had told him. If you don't believe it, that's your business—you're the only one who will suffer the consequences."

"Why did you lie to me about what was in the cylinder?"

"I didn't lie to you," said Rasmus. "I told you as much as you needed to know, enough to make you do what, if you could think of yourself as a proper member of the community, you should have done in any case."

"I'm willing to bet that the cylinder was never stolen from you. That the only time this cylinder was ever stolen was when I stole it."

"I have dozens of lives on my hands to worry about. I have the continuation of a community to attend to, Josef. Even more than that: the continuation of a species. What does it matter, next to that, if you weren't told things in a way that you could clearly understand them? What does it matter, next to that, if the factuality of certain things was, let us say, questionable?"

"You're a bastard," said Horkai.

"No need for name calling," said Rasmus.

"I've fulfilled my part of the bargain," said Horkai. "Now I wash my hands of you."

"Let's wait and see," said Rasmus.

"No," said Horkai. "I'm leaving." He stood and started for the door.

"I still have something you want," said Ramsus.

Horkai stopped, his hand on the knob. "And what might that be?" he asked.

"Knowledge," said Rasmus. "Answers."

And perhaps, of everything, perhaps this was what Horkai regretted most. That upon hearing these words, he turned and returned to his seat instead of going out the door and up the stairs and leaving forever.

29

"ASK ME ANYTHING," SAID RASMUS. "Anything you want. I'll answer your questions honestly."

"Why should I believe you?" asked Horkai.

"Because you don't have any other choice," said Rasmus. "The only person who possibly has answers to your questions is sitting here before you. Either you listen to him or you don't."

Horkai hesitated, finally nodded. "All right," he said. "What was I before the Kollaps?"

"Truly? Nobody knows. My father found you, just as I said, dragged you to safety, nursed you back to health. You never spoke of who you were before or of what you'd done, but whether because then, as now, you had holes in your memory or because you simply didn't want to talk about it, who can say? My father claimed that most everybody was like that in those early days. That everyone had lost enough that you knew better than to talk about it."

"There wasn't anything with me when he found me?"

"No, nothing. It was true what I said before. Everything

you had was burned. It was unimaginable that you yourself survived."

"So I wasn't a fixer? A detective?"

Rasmus shrugged. "Who knows? I suppose you might have been."

"And Horkai's my real name?"

"Horkai's the only name I have for you."

"Why lie to me? Why tell me that I was ill?"

Rasmus hesitated. "I already told you," he finally said, "that's what I heard from my father. If I had the facts wrong, I'm sorry."

"You're still lying," said Horkai.

"Believe what you want," Rasmus said.

"What about the mules?"

"What about them?"

"They kept saying that one of them was first, but insisting that they weren't brothers. What did they mean by that? Why are they mules?"

Rasmus was silent for a time, staring down at his hands. "You're not ready to hear the answer to that," he finally said.

"Who are you to tell me what I'm ready for?"

"Let's just say you're not in the right mind-set."

"Tell me anyway."

And when Rasmus shook his head, Horkai took out his pistol and aimed it at his head.

"More proof that you're not in the right mind-set," said Rasmus, still calm.

"Tell me or I'll shoot," said Horkai.

"If you do that, then who will answer your questions?"

And then Horkai was out of his chair and around the desk. He swung the butt of his pistol, knocked Rasmus and his chair over.

"Tell me," he said again.

Rasmus lay there wincing, a gash on his cheek gushing blood, his eye already starting to swell shut. Even so, Horkai had to hit him again before he would speak.

"Because, like you, they're not really human," he said.

"Not human? How?"

"You were made out there," said Rasmus, gesturing. "Some weird mutation or transformation triggered by the events of the Kollaps. The mules we made here."

"What do you mean, *made*?"

"In a laboratory."

"But they're flesh and blood."

"They're not human. They're grown in a solution. Recycled genetic material, manipulated to provide certain characteristics. They're not so much brothers as slight and deliberate variations of the same being. Sturdy bastards, mules, but not as stable as humans. They're made too quickly. Even without exposure to the outside, they last a decade or two, then start to break down. They're disposable. But we always keep a few new ones at the ready."

"They're genetic experiments," said Horkai.

"They're members of the community," said Rasmus. "The hive. But in the same way a dog is a member of a human family. They know their place, they've been trained to stay in it."

It made him furious. He bent down and slapped Rasmus.

"Told you that you weren't ready," said Rasmus. "You haven't had to live through the aftermath—you slept through it. You haven't had to face facts the way the rest of us have for the last thirty years."

"What's to stop me from killing you?"

"All you're doing with talk like that is proving that

you're an animal, that you shouldn't be let loose," said Rasmus, and he smiled.

Frustrated, Horkai put the gun away, returned to his seat. He leaned his elbows on the table, held his head in his hand. He heard the sound of Rasmus slowly getting up, breathing heavily, then setting his chair aright, sitting in it.

"Feel better?" Rasmus asked, his voice thick with sarcasm.

"I'm going now," he said.

"All right," said Rasmus. "Have it your way."

BUT WHEN HE OPENED THE DOOR, there were Olaf and Oleg, coming back. They shouldered their way past him.

"Should be okay," Olaf said. "Technician says that most won't survive but a few will. Enough to get started."

"All right," said Rasmus. "Have him preserve the rest as well. We'll salvage what material we can."

"What happened to you?" asked Oleg.

"I had a little fall," said Rasmus.

The twins both glanced at Horkai.

"Nothing to worry about," Rasmus said. "A minor disagreement."

"You're going?" asked Olaf.

"I'm going," said Horkai. "I did what you asked."

"No hard feelings," said Rasmus. He held out his hand. When Horkai didn't reach out to take it, he said, "I'm not asking you to be friends. I'm just trying to thank you for what you've done."

Reluctantly, he stretched out his hand, took Rasmus's own. Then he released it and turned and reached for the handle of the door.

And that was the moment they chose to fall upon him.

. . .

HE FELT A HEAVY BLOW on the back of his head, stumbled, and fell into the door. He slid down, felt the door vibrate and crack as it was struck just above his head. He turned and saw Olaf trying to work a hammer out of the wood, with Oleg trying to get past his brother and at him as well. He kicked hard and heard the crack as Oleg's leg gave, the cry as he went down. He looked up and there was the hammer coming down. He turned his head so it glanced off his neck to break or bruise his collarbone. He was fumbling in his pocket, trying to get the gun out, but it was stuck, he couldn't get to it, and the hammer was coming down again. He swept his legs sideward and knocked Olaf's feet out from under him, the hammer striking his arm and making it go numb, all Olaf's weight landing on him. And then he was scrambling, pushing Olaf off, struggling up. He looked up just in time to have the back of a chair splintered over his face.

He went down, groaning, and immediately someone was on him, holding his face down against the ground, immobilizing one of his arms. He tried to roll over with the other arm, but then there were other people on him as well, holding him down, keeping him down, a dozen or more of them. He groaned again.

"Josef," he heard Rasmus's voice hiss in his ear. "So you've decided to stay with us after all."

And then they were tearing his shirt up close to the collar, ripping it open, and someone was pulling the gun out of his pocket, stripping the rifle away, pulling his boots off as well.

"Get the hypodermic," said Rasmus.

"Look what I found in his boot," one of the twins said somewhere above him, either Olaf or Oleg, he couldn't tell which.

"Throw it over with the other weapons," said Rasmus. "And for God's sake, get the hypodermic." And suddenly

Horkai's head was free. He jerked it up, trying to look around, struggling and failing to break free. He roared with frustration. And then others' hands were on his head again, holding it down, grinding it into the floor.

He felt a sharp pricking in his neck, and jerked.

"Hold the bastard still!" yelled Rasmus. "Hold him!"

He felt the pricking again, then briefly an intense coldness followed by a burning and an itching all over his body, and then an intense wave of pain.

He heard someone above him laughing.

He cried out and tried to throw them off, but already his limbs felt thick and distant. He felt the hands leave his head. He tried to lift it and still could, but when he tried to move his hands, they refused to obey him.

And then Rasmus was there in front of him, holding his head off the ground by the hair, still breathing heavily. He bent down so his head was almost touching the ground, so he could look Horkai straight in the eye.

"There," said Rasmus. "As peaceful as a baby." And then struck him in the face, over and over again, until he passed out.

PART FIVE

A SENSATION, AGAIN, OF COMING BACK to life, only not quite that: half life maybe. Still utter darkness, though perhaps a faint hint of light on the horizon. A swirl of memory and imagination, a bloody swath depicting the past, real or imaginary, smeared across the inside of his skull. Bodies everywhere. A light that shone through his skin to reveal his bones. A dead child, a dead wife, and then that, too, blown away in a fine drift of ash. The whole world cut up and churned under and him lying there for days, half-dead, half-alive, waiting for someone to come.

Or no, that wasn't right. A man crawling up an abandoned and devastated freeway, alone. No food, no water, knees and hands bloody, slow and then slower still, and then lying there in a heap, exhausted, waiting to die.

Something fluttered, something scraped, told him—because slowly there was starting to be such a thing as a him—no, that wasn't right either. A man, in the dark, feeling around him for the body of another man he planned to kill. A man, stumbling, striking walls while other men tried to bring him down.

Or a man, frozen, stuffed into a cylinder, unable to move, unable to draw breath, waiting to come back to life again.

Only it wasn't that either, at least he didn't think so.

But he was beginning to have the feeling that when he opened his eyes and saw who was standing over him, he would realize it would be much worse than any of these possibilities.

30

"HE'S COMING AROUND," he heard a voice say. He felt someone slapping his cheeks softly; then his eye was parted and a light shone in and then moved away. He managed, with great effort, to open the eye again, then the other eye as well, saw nothing at first but a blur. It all seemed familiar somehow, as if it had happened before.

Oh, Christ, he thought, without knowing exactly why. *It's starting all over again.*

His head ached. The blur of the sun smeared further and then slowly became clearer and clearer, becoming a light in a concrete ceiling and there, before him, two faces. One was a technician that he vaguely recognized. The other was Rasmus.

"Where am I?" he asked, his voice hardly louder than a whisper. "Did I just come out of storage?"

"No," said Rasmus. "You're just about to go into it."

And then it came rushing back, inexorably. He tried to get up, found he couldn't move more than his head and neck. Rasmus smiled. "You're paralyzed," he said. "Don't you remember?"

"You did this to me," he said.

"Of course I did," said Rasmus.

"But why?"

"Mr. Horkai, you're far too valuable a commodity for us to lose. Every community needs a guardian angel. That's what you are for us. You're our guardian angel, albeit a somewhat reluctant one." His hand moved forward, stroked the side of Horkai's cheek softly. "We don't travel well. You go places we can't. We'll store you until we need you again."

"I won't help you," said Horkai. "Not a second time."

"Not the next time, you mean," he said. "That's the same thing you said before this time. And the same thing you said the time before that. And before that. And yet, given time, a scrambling of the head, and a certain befuddlement, you always come around."

"But you said I was in storage for thirty years."

"You should know by now I don't always tell the truth," said Rasmus. "But yes, in a manner of speaking, you were in storage for thirty years. We just happened to wake you up a few times along the way. But this next time, it may well be thirty years. You've done very well for us this time," he said. "I'm willing to bet it'll be a while before we require your services again."

"I'll never help you," he said. "Next time I wake up, I'll kill you."

Rasmus smiled. "You're nothing if not consistent," he said. "Always the same threat every time." He motioned the technician forward, and the man approached wearing rubber gloves, a wet cotton ball in his hand. He carefully moistened one temple and then the other and then turned away again.

"Traditionally they used to put a cloth in the mouth as well," said Rasmus. "So that the patient wouldn't bite off his tongue. But you have the advantage of being able to grow a new tongue if you bite yours off."

Then the technician was back, holding two metal paddles with insulated handles. He handed them to Rasmus, who took them, pressed them to either side of Horkai's head.

"What are you doing?" demanded Horkai.

"What does it look like we're doing? We're taking steps to help you forget."

"Why?" asked Horkai. "Why do this to me?"

"I've already told you," said Rasmus. "You're a valuable commodity. We own you. Why would we give you up?" He turned to the technician. "Ready?" he asked.

"Let it build up," said the technician. "Another dozen seconds or so."

Rasmus nodded. "I have to admit, there's something else," he said. He leaned closer and for the first time showed Horkai his genuine face, stripped of all trappings, his eyes sharp with hatred. "My father didn't die because he went out to get you. I lied when I said that. My father died because he sat beside you for days nursing you back to health. You're immune to the poison, your body even feeds on it. But you're also a carrier. Any time you go outside, you get a little bit poisonous. When you come back in, you bring it back in with you. Why do you think we have your storage facility so far away from the rest of the community?"

He moved back, his mask in place again, his true face hidden. "And one last thing," he said. "About your legs. You were, of course, right. There's nothing wrong with them. We made all that happen. But of course, by the time you wake up again, you'll have forgotten all about that, too."

He nodded. Horkai suddenly felt his neck and jaw tense, his skull trying to push its way out of his head. He heard a hissing sound, but it took him a moment to realize it was the sound of him breathing through his own clenched teeth. Then as quickly as it had begun it stopped, and he felt the blood pounding in his ears.

"Again," he heard Rasmus say, and felt his neck and jaw tense and roll, saw the flailing of his arm though he couldn't feel it. He tried to keep his mind focused, tried not to forget what had happened to him, what had brought him there, but he felt his thoughts rapidly receding, being replaced by a wincing, screaming pain.

And when it was finished, there was Rasmus, standing over him, paddles in hand, smiling.

"Again," he chanted. "Again. Again. Again."

UNTIL FINALLY HE FOUND HIMSELF being loaded into a tank, being prepared for storage, for perhaps ten years, for perhaps thirty, for perhaps more. As they prepared him, he was trying to remember everything that had happened, trying not to lose track of what were more and more disconnected images, slowly escaping him, fleeing him. He tried to remember, tried to keep track of where he'd gone wrong so that next time they woke him, it'd be different, and was surprised to find that he still had large parts of it in his head. *Maybe next time,* he told himself, *it actually will be different.*

They closed the lid. *Stay focused,* he told himself. *Remember. Remember.*

And then suddenly the lid was open again, revealing Rasmus's swollen face.

"Almost forgot," he said, and injected something into his neck. "One more thing to help you forget," he said.

He felt quickly dizzy, then nauseated, then vaguely confused. "I'll kill you," said Horkai, his voice already sluggish from whatever the drug was.

Rasmus smiled. "Doesn't matter what you say," he said. "You won't kill me, time will. By the time we wake you up again, I'll be an old man or dead."

Then he straightened up. "Now listen very carefully," he said. "Your name is Josef Horkai. You are a member of my community. You love your community dearly and would do anything to serve it and to serve me. My name is Rasmus. I am your leader and your friend."

And then the lid closed. *Fuck him,* thought Horkai. And then thought, *Who?*

WHERE WAS HE? Why did he feel so drowsy? Last thing he remembered was . . . Something terrible happening, what was it again? Fire and ash and houses, corpses everywhere, the screams of the dead. Yes, he remembered that, more or less, but was that really the last thing? Wasn't there something else?

What's wrong with me?

HE LOOKED UP, saw a blurred shape that, by squinting, he was able to make into a lid or cover. He looked down, saw before his chest a convex surface. *Tank,* he thought. Then came the hissing of an air pump.

Ah, he thought, just before the sudden inrush of extreme cold. *I've been in storage. They must just be waking me up.*